JAYNE ANN

GAMBLER'S WOMAN

KRENTZ

WRITING AS STEPHANIE JAMES

HQN™

ISBN-13: 978-0-373-77144-8
ISBN-10:   0-373-77144-4

GAMBLER'S WOMAN

Printed in U.S.A.

Dear Reader,

Those of you who read my books know that these days I write contemporary romantic thrillers as Jayne Ann Krentz, historical romantic suspense as Amanda Quick and futuristics as Jayne Castle. At the start of my career, however, I wrote classic, battle-of-the-sexes style romance using both my Krentz name and the pen name Stephanie James. This volume contains a story from that time.

I want to take this opportunity to thank all of you—new readers as well as those who have been with me from the start. I appreciate your interest in my books.

Sincerely,

Jayne Ann Krentz

GAMBLER'S WOMAN

CHAPTER ONE

THE THIRD TIME THE QUIETLY DANGEROUS man with the eyes of antique gold materialized near a table where she was playing, Alyssa Chandler ruled out coincidence as an explanation. Statistically speaking, given the size of the casino in which she was gambling and the number of people swarming across its huge glittering floor, it just wasn't very likely that the same man would show up in her vicinity on three different occasions in a single hour.

The probability of three such events occurring randomly simply wasn't very high, and Alyssa knew all about probability theory. No, there had to be another explanation for the man's appearance, and none of the explanations Alyssa could think of sounded very pleasant. All, in fact, sounded rather dangerous; just like the man himself. It was time to move on.

Smiling at the professionally polite blackjack dealer, Alyssa scooped a hundred dollars' worth of chips into her soft, sequined evening clutch. Her carefully draped, off-the-shoulder gown of black jersey swirled gently around her ankles as she turned to slip into the crowd of pleasure seekers. A thin, liquid stream of silver edged the neckline, cuffs and rippling hemline of the dress, subtly reflecting the glow of the chandeliers as Alyssa made her way through the crowd.

The silver trim of the dress wasn't the only thing on her person that reflected the light. A rich fire buried in the depths of her thick auburn hair occasionally caught the elegant glow of the casino fixtures. Parted simply in the middle, the shoulder-length mass fell in a gentle curve on each side of her face, lightly brushing the smooth skin bared by the gown. The auburn hair framed an intelligent, if not beautiful face that was highlighted by a pair of eyes the color of the sea at dawn: not quite green, not quite gray. It was the shimmering awareness in those eyes, together with the charm of a mouth that curved readily into a smile, that made an onlooker forget that the face, as a whole, could not be labeled beautiful.

There was a certain charm to the secret smile that always lurked in her sea-green eyes, and that charm made people overlook the fact that they never knew quite why Alyssa was smiling so subtly. There was charm, too, in the smattering of freckles across her small nose, although tonight she had made a vain attempt to hide that unsophisticated feature. Tonight she was in Las Vegas, dressed in the most expensive gown she could afford, wearing a pair of black leather sandals trimmed at the heel in silver, and she had decided that freckles did not particularly go with the persona of elegant lady gambler that she had adopted.

If one ignored the freckles, however, it could be said that the rest of her fit rather well into the image she had constructed. Thanks to five feet, seven inches of height and a lot of swimming, the body, cloaked so sleekly in the black dress, was slender and graceful. There was a gentle invitation in the small curves of her high breasts and softly flaring hips; nothing blatant or voluptuous on the grand Las Vegas scale but something that would definitely be evident to the eyes of the discerning. Tonight, Alyssa had dressed to make the most of her figure in a discreet, sophisticated manner.

Knowing the image she was projecting, she would ordinarily have assumed that the man with the golden eyes was merely responding to that subtle, feminine magic. In the minds of the vast majority of the male population, the illusion of Las Vegas was woven not only with the promise of gambling but with the promise of easily available women.

But the man who had materialized near her three times during the course of the evening had not been focusing on the curve of bared shoulder or narrow waist. He had been watching her play blackjack, and the shuttered fascination in his eyes was far more dangerous to her than lust would have been.

Lust could be handled, firmly and coolly denied with the knowledge that the casino personnel would be only too quick to come to the aid of a patron in distress. For although she had dressed to suit her own fantasy this evening, the intelligent, sensible woman hidden in the black jersey gown had no intention of becoming some *man*'s fantasy. No, a man who might have decided to try his luck with her instead of the roulette wheel would have been no danger.

But a man who followed every move she made when she played blackjack was in another category altogether. Such a man might be very dangerous, indeed.

Was he on the casino's staff? Behind the dealers roamed a variety of personnel who kept an eye on operations: floormen, pit bosses, shift bosses and the casino manager. Most were easily identifiable and certainly made no effort to conceal themselves. But that didn't mean there might not be additional personnel who, like the shills, were supposed to blend in with the patrons.

Slipping through the crowd, Alyssa passed one kind of gambler after another. The traditional figure of the little old lady in tennis shoes stood amid a row of slot machines, industriously throwing away her social security check. A high-rolling, loudmouthed Oklahoma oilman threw his money away with a great deal more showmanship at the craps table. In between ranged every type of gambling human under the sun.

The soft glow of the chandeliers fell impartially on all, reflecting the warmth with which the casino welcomed each customer. That welcome was extended because the vast majority had one thing in common: ultimately, they would all be losers.

There was only one sort of client the casino did not welcome, and that was the very rare individual who won, not just occasionally but consistently, steadily, inevitably. And that was the sort of gambler Alyssa Chandler was. She won.

Oh, she was careful about it, never letting greed carry her away to the extent that the casino management would be alerted. She made it a point to lose periodically, and when she won, it was always in small amounts. But by the time she was ready to leave Las Vegas at the end of the weekend, she planned on being a thousand dollars ahead. There was no reason to think her plans would not be fulfilled. After all, she had made the same decision the weekend before and had gone back to California with precisely a thousand dollars in her purse, all of which had been won in small, discreet sums at several casinos.

Surely she hadn't won enough tonight or been so conspicuous as to attract the unwanted attention of the casino management. A small frown knitted her auburn eyebrows as she moved up the three steps that separated the huge gaming floor from the cocktail lounges and hotel facilities that ringed it. Still, it paid to be cautious. A suspicious casino could easily bar her from playing, and that was the last thing she wanted. Perhaps it was time to get into a cab and head for another establishment.

Debating her course of action as she walked to the lobby area of the hotel casino, Alyssa didn't see the golden-eyed man until he stepped away from the cluster of cheerful gamblers moving into the nearest of the cocktail lounges. Quite suddenly, he was blocking her path.

Alyssa caught her breath as she met his gaze directly for the first time. In that moment, she realized the futility of trying to avoid the confrontation.

"It's all right," he said quietly as if he could read her mind. "I don't work for the casino." The voice was rich, dark and infinitely disturbing.

Relief was Alyssa's first emotion, followed almost immediately by a host of new suspicions and questions. Or was he lying to her about not working for the management? "I can't see why that should be important to me one way or the other," she managed sweetly. "Now, if you'll excuse me, I'm on my way out."

He didn't move. "I'd like to buy you a drink." The tawny gold eyes held hers with an expressionless promise. Alyssa got the distinct impression that it would be risky to turn down his offer of a drink.

For a long moment, they stood in a tableau, assessing each other, playing a waiting game; then, without a word, Alyssa decided to capitulate and find out what he wanted. There was no point in running away. If she had been marked by the casino, she had been marked. Better to find out exactly what this man wanted. Ignorance was never really bliss; it could often be downright dangerous. With a faint inclination of her head, she turned and walked into the nearby lounge.

He followed, a dark, silent shadow at her heels, taking her arm just as she located an empty table and was about to sit down. His touch, warm through the fabric of her dress, surprised her, drawing her attention briefly to his hands as he took the seat across from her. Long, well-shaped fingers gave an impression of strength and exquisite sensitivity. In the next instant, Alyssa was shocked to find herself wondering what those fingers would feel like on a woman's naked skin. She banished the image with the single-minded skill of a professional statistician who knew how to focus on the big picture.

"Have you finished playing for the evening, or would you like to stick with the mineral water you've been drinking?" the stranger inquired very politely.

Alyssa winced. He had even noticed what she had been drinking! "I've finished for the evening," she told him coolly. "I'll have a Drambuie."

"With the glass warmed?"

"Please." His politeness was beginning to ruffle her nerves. Such polished civility, such courtesy, such an expression of urbane attention, had to be suspect in a man, any man.

While he gave their order to the pretty cocktail waitress, Alyssa made a quick, surreptitious survey of her accoster. A pelt of dark, Vandyke-brown hair was combed easily back from a broad forehead and worn long enough to brush the collar of his crisp white shirt. His eyes, the feature Alyssa had been most aware of for the past hour, were of a light amber brown that bore more than a passing resemblance to the color of old gold. Those eyes bothered Alyssa, primarily because she failed utterly to read any expression in them other than the suspect politeness.

The remainder of his face had been carved with a blunt chisel. Strong, harsh planes formed the aggressive nose and the line of an unyielding jaw. Alyssa decided he must have been in his late thirties, probably perilously close to forty, judging by the lines of experience that marked him. She herself had just reached the magic number of thirty. At least there was no gray yet in her hair, she realized with hidden amusement, noting the silver at the stranger's temples.

The white shirt he wore was clearly of excellent craftsmanship, pleated in the tuxedo style and buttoned up the front with tiny black studs. A discreet black bow tie circled the strong lines of his throat under the collar.

The jacket and close-fitting slacks in a sober shade of dark charcoal were as immaculately tailored as the shirt.

The lines of his body beneath the evening clothes were lean and hard, reminding Alyssa of a prowling wolf. In her high-heeled sandals, she stood nearly five feet, nine inches, but there was no denying she'd felt physically dominated by his body as he'd escorted her into the lounge. It wasn't that he was so much taller than she—Alyssa guessed his height at around five feet, ten or eleven inches—but there was a strength and power in him that made an impact on her senses. Alyssa wasn't at all sure she liked the feeling. It made her even more wary than she already was.

"Like you, I never drink while I'm working," the stranger said as he finished giving the cocktail order and sat back in his seat. The firm line of his mouth tilted upward fractionally in a polite smile. "But since we've both come to the end of a hard night's labor, I think we deserve something more substantial than mineral water." Alyssa had heard him order Scotch for himself.

"You'll excuse me, I'm sure," she began evenly, "but I really haven't the vaguest idea of what you're talking about or why you wish to buy me a drink." Might as well go on the offensive, she decided grimly.

"I'm sorry"—the man apologized at once, his golden eyes reflecting no genuine measure of regret—

"I haven't introduced myself yet, have I? I'm Jordan Kyle."

He arched a dark brow in polite inquiry, inviting her to respond to his introduction by offering her own name. She did so with a saccharine civility that mocked his own. "Alyssa."

Jordan Kyle waited a moment, and then, when no further name was forthcoming, he asked gently, "Just Alyssa?"

"Isn't it enough?"

He sighed. "I meant what I said earlier. You don't have to be afraid of me. I don't work for the casino."

"Is that supposed to be reassuring? Why should I worry about whether or not you work here?" Alyssa tried to say flippantly as the drinks arrived. "I haven't been cheating," she added when the waitress had disappeared.

"No, but you've been winning. When and where you please."

Alyssa's fingers tightened around the snifter of Drambuie, but she didn't think she gave any other outward sign of her tension. Opening her sea-green eyes innocently wide, she smiled. "I've also been losing."

"That, too, seems to happen when and where you please," he drawled.

"Are you accusing me of cheating?" Alyssa demanded, genuine outrage etching her words.

"Not at all," he denied softly. "I've been watching

you all evening, and the only thing I could accuse you of is turning what is supposed to be a game of chance into a business. There aren't very many people in the whole world who can do that, Alyssa. I know."

Her gaze collided with his. "How do you know?"

"Because I do exactly the same thing for a living."

Don't panic, Alyssa instructed herself. Just keep calm. And above all, don't admit to anything! "I'm sure the casino would be very interested to hear that, Mr. Kyle, but I really don't see why you should be telling me."

He hesitated a moment, assessing her mildly confused expression, and then he grinned. The gleaming flash of masculine laughter lasted only a moment before it dissolved back into a polite smile, but in that moment, Alyssa was aware of an inexplicable desire to match his humor with her own. It was as if a kindred spirit had briefly reached across the gulf that separates most people and invited her to join in the game of laughing at the rest of the world. Before she could comprehend exactly what had happened, Jordan was saying smoothly, "And now I know why you don't play poker. You undoubtedly have the talent, but your eyes would broadcast your hand every time."

"Who are you, Mr. Kyle?"

"I've told you. Just another professional. How long are you going to be here in Vegas?" He sipped his drink, watching her over the rim of the glass.

"I'm only here for the weekend," Alyssa said firmly.

"Contrary to what you keep implying, I am definitely not a professional gambler. I have a full-time job back in California, and I come to Las Vegas for the same reason everybody else does. For fun."

"And for the money. How much did you win tonight in all? A couple of hundred dollars?"

"That's hardly any of your business!" Alyssa leaned back in her chair, trying to appear totally casual, totally unconcerned. But her pulse was still racing as she tried to figure out exactly who Jordan Kyle was.

"I like the way you do it. You're not greedy. As long as you're not greedy and as long as you don't feel the urge to tell anyone else what you can do with numbers and cards, you should be fine. Of course, sooner or later, it will probably be wise to give Vegas a break and do a little traveling. No sense taking undue risks."

"A little traveling?" she prompted, more than willing to let him do the talking.

"Ummm. Atlantic City, Europe, Monte Carlo, the Bahamas, Puerto Rico. It's a big world for people like us, Alyssa. Or haven't you discovered that yet?"

"I'm afraid I haven't done much traveling," she admitted cautiously, wondering at the twist in the conversation. "Are you suggesting I, uh, leave town?"

He shook his head, mouth twisting in wry amusement. "You really are nervous about me, aren't you? For the last time, I am not in the employ of this casino, and I am not politely suggesting you leave town. But

I am going to suggest that now that your evening's work is done, you spend your time off with me."

"Why?" she challenged bravely, more confused than ever. Was he merely trying to pick her up, after all? Or was this some elaborate scheme of the casino's security system? But that didn't make sense, really. If the casino was suspicious, wouldn't its representative simply tell her to leave? She wasn't quite sure how things like that worked, but she doubted that the management would pussyfoot around about it. In Nevada, the casinos made the rules, and they didn't bother to apologize for them.

"Because," Jordan answered gently, "I'm a man who happens to be alone tonight and you're a woman in the same situation. Furthermore, we seem to have something in common. Can you think of any better reasons?" His polite, expressionless gaze roved over her face and then fell to the expanse of throat and shoulder left visible by the black and silver dress. Alyssa felt the heat of the molten gold and sensed the unexpected excitement it was generating within her. What was this man doing to her tonight? She never paired off with anyone when she came to Las Vegas, preferring to live out her gambling-world fantasy in private. Most of the men she encountered in the casinos were totally uninteresting, anyway, caught up as they were in the strange fever that was true gambling. They weren't playing the way she played, and that single fact put a tremendous distance between herself and the people around her. But this man seemed to know that she was able to do something different at the tables, and the fact that he had guessed that much intrigued her.

"I only won a couple of hundred dollars," she heard herself point out carefully. "Anyone can get lucky and win that much in an evening. It's nothing."

He regarded her enigmatically and then answered the unspoken question. "You want me to tell you how I came to realize you're not relying on luck? I'm not sure I can explain it completely. I think I noticed you first because there was an aura of calm certainty about you when you played. As if the issue was never in doubt. When you occasionally lost, you looked as coolly satisfied as when you won, and I knew it must have been because the losses were deliberate. I found myself very curious and very interested. Then I started watching carefully while you played."

Alyssa shivered, remembering the feel of those golden eyes on her. An appalling thought made her ask, "Do you think anyone else noticed?"

"No," he reassured her with a smile. "In this whole roomful of people, there's probably not another soul who would have noticed anything other than the fact that you were alone. As they say, Alyssa, it takes one to know one." He saluted her briefly with his glass. "Come and spend some time with me, lady gambler.

A casino can be the loneliest place on earth for people like us."

"I'm not lonely," she whispered, caught by the fleeting wistfulness that came and went so quickly in his eyes. This man was lonely?

"I am," he returned simply. "And I would very much like to spend some time talking shop with someone who *understands*."

Alyssa swallowed uneasily, knowing the oddest sensation of being seduced. It was ridiculous, Jordan Kyle was a man she would normally have ignored completely. He was definitely not a part of her real world, and the people of her casino fantasy world were never allowed to step past the invisible boundaries she erected. Yet here he was, reaching through the illusion and tearing aside the barriers. The real excitement of the night world that had always intrigued her had never been so close.

"I don't know you," she whispered, unable to look away from his gaze.

"You will," he promised quietly. "As soon as you stop worrying about who I might be, you'll realize who I really am."

"And who is that?" Alyssa felt strangely breathless as she waited for his response. The lure he was casting was snagging her, pulling at her. She didn't begin to understand the spell being woven around her by this man, but it was as real as anything had ever been in her life.

"Come spend some time with me and discover the answer for yourself," he murmured persuasively.

Alyssa frowned, common sense asserting itself for a moment. "I'm not interested in being a bed partner for you or any other man, Jordan. That's not why I come to Las Vegas."

"I know that's not what brought you here. How much do you plan to take home with you?" he added matter-of-factly.

For some reason, the question goaded her. "A thousand dollars," she tossed back, her expression defying him to laugh.

Jordan Kyle didn't laugh. He nodded as if that were the most normal goal in the world and then asked, "Saving up for something special?"

It was Alyssa's turn to smile. "A down payment on the most beautiful red Porsche you ever saw in your life!" Her sea-colored eyes lit with inner laughter. She didn't need the Porsche. No one really needed a luxury like that. What was necessary was to have some goal for the money she was winning. Her original goal, the one that had first brought her to Las Vegas, had been satisfied when she had won enough money to pay her friend Julia's maternity bills. But by the time that had been accomplished, Alyssa had discovered that she was intrigued by this new, unreal world of the night.

It was always night in a Las Vegas casino. The patrons were carefully shielded from such distractions as light and fresh air and wall clocks. "What about you?" she decided to challenge.

He lowered his dark lashes consideringly. "What am I saving my winnings for? Nothing special. Just making a living." And then the flashing grin appeared once more for an instant. "I already bought my Porsche."

Alyssa found herself smiling in response. The spell Jordan Kyle was weaving grew more dangerous, and she was rapidly becoming more and more oblivious to the menace. Las Vegas was a city of illusion, and for the first time she sensed she could do more than pretend she was a part of it. With this man, she could find out what it was like to truly immerse herself in it.

"What else have you bought with your winnings, Jordan?"

He shrugged offhandedly. "A house on the Oregon coast, the Porsche, the clothes I'm wearing, my last meal, plane fares to Reno and Monte Carlo. You name it. Everything I've owned since I got out of the army. Winning is how I support myself, Alyssa. Don't you understand? Gambling is my livelihood."

She blinked, a little taken aback. "That's *all* you do for a living? Gamble?"

"And win," he reminded her gently. "As a means of financial support, it doesn't work very well unless you win."

"Your...your family doesn't mind what you do for a living?" If her father had lived to see how she was entertaining herself these days, he would have been appalled. If she had actually started to gamble for a living, he probably would have disowned her entirely. It made her uneasy to think about it even though he was gone.

"I have no immediate family. My parents were killed when I was very young, and there is no one else who would particularly care," he explained neutrally. "Does your family know what you're doing these days?" he added, mouth crooking.

She shook her head. "No. My parents were divorced years ago. I was raised by my father after my mother left to marry another man. My father was killed a couple of years ago, and I rarely see my mother." But she didn't want to get into a discussion of that nature. Deliberately, she turned back to the original topic. "You really don't have any trouble winning?"

"No more than you do."

"You don't—" she broke off, searching for a more polite word and couldn't find it. "You don't cheat?"

"Cheating in a well-run casino would be infinitely more difficult than winning our way," he drawled easily. "And less reliable."

"Not to mention rather dangerous," she murmured. "Some of these pit bosses and floormen look like they wouldn't be very understanding about cheating."

Jordan flicked his well-shaped hand dismissively. "They're professionals in their own way. Here in Nevada, at least, they run the house in an honest fashion, and they intend to keep the client honest, too."

"No reason why they shouldn't run things honestly when they can figure on taking twenty percent of the drop every day of the year!" The "drop" was the total amount bet by customers in a casino. It was figured on a daily basis, year in, year out. The numbers were staggeringly large and the profit correspondingly so.

"How long have you been treating yourself to spare cash in Vegas, Alyssa?" Jordan asked.

She paused before answering, wary once again at the pointed question. But what did it matter if she told him the truth? He'd already guessed most of it. "A few months ago, I decided to take what I know about math and statistics and see what happened. To tell you the truth, I was astonished. My knowledge of probability theory gave me a solid understanding of the math behind gambling, but once I started, I discovered I seemed to have a certain…a certain intuition—" She broke off, shrugging. "As I said, I was amazed. I had no idea it would be so easy."

"It isn't for most people," he reminded her. "And the only reason you're getting away with it is because you have the sense not to get greedy. You don't call attention to yourself as a consistent winner. You're playing it smart."

"What about you? Have you really been doing the same thing for years?" Alyssa was a little awed at the notion of supporting oneself completely by gambling. His ability in mathematics, especially probability theory, must be as good as her own. And he must have that extra thing she'd labeled intuition.

"I've had a head for numbers since I was a kid," he replied negligently. "Playing cards and rolling dice were natural outlets for that kind of skill in the neighborhood where I grew up."

"What about school? Have you had much in the way of mathematics?" Her curiosity was growing. Alyssa leaned forward, cupping her snifter in both hands to lift it to her lips while she waited.

"Only what I've picked up on my own. It's easy to get in to audit university classes, and I do that when I need specific instruction or guidance." His mouth twisted wryly. "If we're going to sit here and swap educational backgrounds, I'm afraid I will definitely come out the loser. You, I take it, have a lot of formal training?"

She lifted her bare shoulder in a small shrug. "I'm a statistician. I've got a degree in math."

"Where do you work?"

"In California." This time her answer was clipped. She still wasn't sure how much she could trust Jordan Kyle. No sense giving him unnecessary details.

"California." He nodded, accepting that. "But you're here for the weekend?"

"Yes." She waited, inwardly surprised by the breathless feeling of expectation.

He moved suddenly, leaning across the table to cradle her hands in his own as she held the snifter. His golden gaze flowed over her, trapping her. "Will you spend your weekend with me, lady gambler? I want very much to get to know you better. Do you realize you may be the only woman in the entire world to whom I can really talk?" This last was said on a whimsical, captivating note.

Alyssa felt a small tremor go through her and tried to rally her defenses. "A moment ago, you only wanted to spend the remainder of the evening with me."

"Okay, I'll settle for that. At the end of the evening, we can discuss the rest of the weekend."

"You're very persistent," she tried to say lightly, fiercely aware of the strong, sensitive hands cupping hers. In this pose, they must appear to be lovers to those around them, she realized a little wildly. "And you frighten me."

"I know. But I think you're a very daring sort of woman," he said with a smile. "Don't forget, I've been watching you play cards for the past two hours. I know a great deal about you, Alyssa. Come with me tonight and I'll show you my world."

"I've already seen your world."

"I think you've only dropped in long enough to play occasionally. Tonight I'll show you much, much more." Jordan was abruptly on his feet, removing the snifter from her hands and placing it on the small table.

"Jordan?"

But her small protest was overridden. "Hush, partner. It's you and me against the world. Can't you see that? We're not like anybody else here in Vegas because we come to play the games on our own terms. But we can have fun on our own terms, too!" He captured her wrist in a warm grip that sent a thrill through her and strode out of the cocktail lounge, towing her in his wake.

"Jordan, please!" Alyssa didn't know whether to laugh or scream for help. Before she could make up her mind, she was being whisked out the door and into one of the cabs lined up in front of the casino. Jordan was rattling off the name of another famous establishment before he had shut the car door. Hearing the destination and knowing she would be safe on the premises of such a major hotel casino, Alyssa gave up the small battle and collapsed back into the seat. Across the small distance separating them, she eyed her abductor with a mocking gaze. "Do you have references?"

"Sorry, in my business, references would be disastrous," he said, chuckling. "I cultivate anonymity. The only guarantee I can give you is my word as a professional gambler that I'll take care of you tonight."

"Do you do this sort of thing often?"

"Kidnap lady gamblers? No, not often. But then I haven't encountered one quite like you before. Ah, here we are."

The cab deposited them beneath the lights of a glittering casino complex, and Jordan escorted Alyssa into the orderly confusion of gamblers, slot machines and cocktail lounges.

"Here, put a quarter in one of the slots," he instructed, handing her the coin.

She took it, arching an eyebrow in surprise. "You play the slots? Everyone knows they're almost as bad as a state-run lottery! The odds against the player are incredible. For heaven's sake! The house mechanics deliberately set them to pay out only what the house wants paid out!"

"Alyssa, my sweet," he explained easily as he urged her toward the nearest bank of slot machines. "I don't play the slots to win."

"Then why…?"

"I play them for luck," he said, smiling.

"Luck!" Now she truly was startled. "You believe in luck?"

"When you've seen as much of this world as I have, you'll discover that like it or not, there is an element of luck in the universe. Play the slot, Alyssa. Tonight I feel lucky."

Lips curving in quiet laughter, Alyssa plunked the quarter into the hungry machine and pulled the handle.

The colorful wheels spun madly, and then, to her surprise, two quarters cascaded into the small pan beneath the bandit. She scooped them up and handed them to Jordan with a flourish.

"Your winnings, sir!"

"What did I tell you? Tonight I am a lucky man. No more work, however. We're here to play." He took her arm and walked her through the crowd thronging the gambling floor. "There's an excellent group in the lounge."

Alyssa knew later that she would never forget that night. It was a fantasy come to life. She moved through the exotic world of the Las Vegas illusion on the arm of a man who seemed to have materialized from it. They didn't play at the tables, although they occasionally watched others gamble and spoke softly about the odds of various games, the house edge, the bewildering variety of people who came to throw their money away joyously.

Through it all, Alyssa sensed a growing feeling of companionship, a closeness to this stranger. Jordan Kyle viewed the world of cards and dice exactly as she did, as a complex set of problems in probability that could be manipulated to a certain extent by those rare individuals who had the intuitive feel for the math involved. Instead of being the victims of the wild ups and downs of chance that hypnotized the average player, they were in control of their luck. That single fact proved a bond. They were different from the rest, a man and a woman with a shared talent.

Jordan Kyle moved in his world with the subtle confidence of a man who knows he can control it, his firm grip on Alyssa telling her that he considered her his intellectual mate in this dazzling, glittering sphere.

That realization brought up the inevitable question of whether or not Jordan was also seeking in her another kind of mate.

The question was answered when he took her into his arms on the dance floor.

CHAPTER TWO

"CAN WE TALK ABOUT THE REST OF THE WEEKEND now?" The rich, dark voice was a deeply seductive whisper as Jordan pressed his mouth lightly against Alyssa's hair. "Or at least the rest of the night? You must realize by now that I want you, honey."

She was a little startled by the fine trembling she sensed in the hand that rested possessively against the small of her back. Alyssa doubted that there was very much that could cause Jordan Kyle to reveal any inner turmoil he might be experiencing. He'd had far too much practice wearing the polite, remote façade he used in this dangerous, glittering world he called home. The knowledge that she had the power to make his control slip even a little was deeply seductive in itself.

"I'd rather not talk about anything except the present," she breathed. But her arms lifted to circle his neck, and her head found a natural place against the charcoal-gray shoulder of his evening jacket.

"Do you think the future will cease to exist just

because you insist on dealing only with the present?" She could feel his strong, sensitive fingers on her back, moving with ravishing awareness, sending a thrill of almost feline pleasure up her spine. Such wonderful hands, Alyssa thought vaguely.

"The future will arrive in due course. Why anticipate it?"

"When you work with probability theory the way we do, Alyssa, the future is always a factor," Jordan growled half humorously.

"Because the mathematics of chance rest on the concept of an infinite future?" she teased. "It may be true that the probable outcome of a spin of the roulette wheel can be calculated only because there are, in theory, an infinite number of spins which can be made," she went on in a lecturing tone. "But I," she added with mocking demureness, "am not a roulette wheel."

"Meaning I can't possibly calculate my chances of having you in my bed tonight?"

"Precisely. Save your mental energy for the gambling tables where the laws of probability apply." Alyssa lifted her head, gray-green eyes sparkling with mischief. Her lips parted in a gently taunting smile that drew his gaze like a magnet.

In the next instant, the mockery was being kissed from her mouth. Jordan had signaled no warning of his intentions, and he found her mouth vulnerable and invitingly open in the soft curve of a smile. He seized the opportunity with the single-minded will of a man who respects the laws of chance too much not to take advantage of a bit of luck.

Alyssa's eyes opened wide as his mouth closed forcefully, warmly over hers. She hadn't been expecting the kiss; not here, not yet. The future was upon her.

And it seemed to envelop her. She felt her senses spin, making her feel rather like a roulette wheel, after all. At the mercy of chance instead of in control of it, Alyssa could rally no defense. The touch of his mouth was firm and heated and deeply demanding. She felt unable to do anything other than let the professional gambler determine the rules of the game.

Slowly, inevitably, he forced her head back while he explored the unknown territory behind her lips. As the languid strains of the music swirled around them on the shadowy dance floor, Jordan probed the delicate flower of her mouth with his tongue. Even as he mastered her lips, his exquisitely erotic touch was working magic in the deliciously sensitive area at the base of her spine.

"Alyssa," he grated against her mouth, "my sweet lady gambler. Do you know what you do to me? What you've been doing to me all evening? I've never wanted a woman as suddenly, as completely, as I want you tonight."

The barely restrained passion of his words touched

her senses as deliberately as his fingers stroked the curve of her hip, and Alyssa sighed as her mouth was freed. When he feathered the smallest of kisses on her temple, she turned her lips instinctively against his throat. The shudder that went through him as she began to respond was accompanied by a husky groan. Jordan's hold on her tightened.

"Jordan?" The question in her single word was fraught with a million uncertainties, all ancient and all female.

"Hush, sweetheart. There is only the present for you tonight, remember?"

Alyssa knew she was being seduced, and she could only wonder at it. She was thirty years old, and never had she experienced anything quite like this, not even during the short, disastrous period of her marriage to an awesomely brilliant mathematician. It fascinated and hypnotized and lured and promised. She had attempted to live a reasonably normal, if somewhat restrained, social life since her divorce. But always she maintained a sense of control over any given situation. No, never in her whole life had she known the true sensation of outright seduction. Was this the peril involved when illusion became reality?

The dance slowly drifted to a conclusion, leaving Alyssa feeling as unsteady as if she had been drinking far too much. There was no need to worry about how she would make it back to the table, however; Jordan's arm was anchored securely around her waist, and she was pinned tightly against the side of his lean, warm body.

"Another Drambuie for my lady and another Scotch for me," Jordan murmured to the hovering cocktail waitress as he carefully seated Alyssa.

"Are you plying me with drink?" Alyssa demanded interestedly.

"Don't fret," he said, sitting down next to her and reaching out to cover her hand with his own. "I don't intend to get you drunk." The pad of his thumb traced a tantalizing line across the sensitive skin of her inner wrist. When Alyssa silently caught her breath, he cradled her hand in his fingers and lifted it to his lips for a fleeting caress.

"You've been spending too much time on the Continent," Alyssa informed him with an attempt at lightness as she retrieved her hand. Propping her elbow on the table, she rested her chin in the palm he had just kissed. His eyes met hers, and now she could clearly read the desire in them.

"Alyssa, are you going to play games with me tonight?"

"Why not? We're both so good at games of chance," she mocked, feeling an overwhelming desire to bait and tease. It wasn't at all her normal style, but she was beyond questioning her own behavior now.

"Ah." He nodded as if he understood exactly what

she was doing. "I must warn you that I feel an over-powering need to win tonight."

"Meaning you might resort to cheating?"

"Will that be necessary?" The eyes of antique gold seemed to shimmer for a moment as he searched her expression.

"Yes, no, maybe. Do you expect me to go to bed with you when I hardly even know you?"

"Yes, no, maybe," he retorted softly. "I only know I want you." He paused. "I take that back. I know something else. I know I need you tonight. Come upstairs with me, Alyssa."

"Upstairs?"

"I have a room in this hotel," he explained, watching her intently.

"But I'm staying in the hotel where I met you," she began, feeling strangely confused by the accelerated pace at which the evening of illusion was beginning to move.

"You won't need anything. I'll supply everything you ask for tonight, Alyssa. Take a chance and trust me, honey."

"I never take chances when I can't calculate the odds," she made herself say deliberately. Yet she was longing to take his hand and go with him. The sweet desire to abandon herself to fate this evening was growing with every second that passed.

"I can't seem to calculate the odds tonight, either,"

Jordan drawled softly, leaning forward to brush the lightest of kisses against the tip of her nose. "We'll go into this game evenly matched."

"You mean evenly uncertain about the outcome," she countered.

"Haven't you ever wondered what it really means to take a genuine gamble? One where you can't predict the final card in the deck?"

"I find the thought a little frightening," she admitted, unable to look away from his gaze.

"But you're a daring lady gambler, remember? Come with me, Alyssa, and we'll find out together what chance has in store for us." As if he knew the depths of the spell he had cast, Jordan didn't wait for an answer. Tossing the cash on the table for the drinks they had not finished, he stood up and tugged Alyssa up beside him.

Without another word, he guided her through the lounge, out across the wide casino floor and over to the elevators on the far side. In a sensually taut silence, they traveled to the high reaches of the huge hotel. When the elevator doors opened onto a wide hallway decorated in the typically ornate Las Vegas style, Alyssa hung back for a moment. Then Jordan was gently crowding her out into the thickly carpeted hall.

"Don't think about the future, sweetheart," he coaxed huskily. "Just think about how much I need you tonight." His arm around her waist was binding, the palm of his hand against her hip a heated branding iron that burned through the thin material of the draped black dress.

"Jordan?" She turned a questioning face up to him as he brought them to a halt in front of one of the doors.

"You'll have to forgive the room, honey," he said on a note of wry humor as he shoved the key into the lock. "I didn't have much choice!"

"The room? But I... Oh!"

Alyssa stared in shock as he opened the door and switched on the light. "Oh, my goodness," she managed before the laughter overtook her. "I had no idea there was anything like this available! My room is quite ordinary."

"Anything is available in Vegas for a price, but I give you my word I didn't request this." Jordan grimaced ruefully as he shut the door with quiet firmness. "The front desk said it was all they had left."

It was undoubtedly some decorator's fantasy of a room devoted to passion. Everything appeared to be done in red—heavy, plush bordello red. The bed was round and elevated on a red-carpeted pedestal. There was a round canopy above lined with a round mirror. Red velvet drapes framed the view of the endless Las Vegas night, and one wall was done in mirrors. A wallpaper design in red velvet and gold foil dominated the opposite wall.

"I'm afraid to go peek in the bathroom!" Alyssa

managed between giggles. The laughter shone in her eyes as she watched him cross the room toward her. For some reason, humor was an excellent release for the tension that had been building within her from the moment when she had first become aware of those golden eyes. She clung to the uneasy laughter as if it could save her.

"Equally tacky, I'm afraid," Jordan said regretfully as he fitted his hands to the bare curve of her shoulders. "No one has ever accused Las Vegas of having taste. Plenty of flash and glitter but not taste!"

"You're going to stand there and claim you didn't deliberately request this room for purposes of seduction?" Alyssa demanded innocently, desperately trying to keep the small joke alive. Anything now to stall the inevitable.

A dull red stained the high bones of his cheeks. "Dear God, no! How could I have guessed I'd be lucky enough to find you tonight?" Jordan rasped, hauling her close and forbidding any further mockery by sealing her mouth with his own.

In an instant, the brief flare of humor was gone, evaporated beneath the heat of Jordan's kiss. Alyssa forgot all about the garish room, the exotic world of the casino twenty stories below, the future and the past. Right now there could only be Jordan Kyle and the passion he was offering. Illusion or not, Alyssa surrendered to it.

"Jordan, oh, Jordan…" His name was a sigh on her lips as he freed her mouth to begin a fiery trail of stinging kisses down the line of her throat. Alyssa's questing fingers slid up from the firm breadth of his shoulders to tangle in the dark depths of his hair. Deliberately, she drew the frosted flames of her nails through the inviting pelt, glorying in the shudder that passed from her body through his.

"Don't think about anything else except us," he commanded thickly, moving his palms along her slender back. Every inch of her was being molded against the strength of him, and when he at last cupped the roundness of her buttocks in his hands and lifted her boldly into his hips, Alyssa sucked in her breath.

"I never intended anything like this to happen," she heard herself whisper dazedly, pressing her face into his jacket. The intoxicating male scent of him tantalized her nostrils. It seemed to be comprised of a hint of spicy aftershave and the natural musk of his body.

"I know, sweetheart, I know," he soothed, and then the gently probing touch of his fingers located the long zipper in the black and silver dress. The fabric began to part, and Alyssa felt the coolness of her back as the fastening was slowly undone.

Suddenly, vividly conscious of the mirrors lining the wall behind her, she stirred in his arms. "Jordan, wait. I…all these mirrors," she ended lamely, not daring to lift her face from the shelter of his jacket.

"I want to see you. All of you." One hand lifted to circle her throat and raised her chin. For a timeless moment, his eyes searched hers, asking questions she couldn't begin to unravel, and then he kissed her.

Under the spell of the deep, drugging kiss, Alyssa stood submissively as the black gown cascaded lightly over her hips to fall into a soft heap at her feet. Then she remembered the outrageous underwear she had bought to go with the dress. My God! She must look right at home here in this gaudy room.

Deeply embarrassed at the thought of how she must appear in the strapless black silk demibra and infinitesimal panties, Alyssa tried to step back. The two wisps of enticement were iced in black lace and had been bought in an attempt to complete her private fantasy. She had never intended any man to see them!

"What's the matter, honey?" Jordan's fingers moved persuasively, gentling her as he sensed the shift in her mood.

"These, uh, things," she began awkwardly, flicking a disparaging gesture down her own almost-nude body and aware she was blushing rather vividly. "I didn't... That is, I don't want you to think I normally dress like this. I mean, they sort of went with the gown and..." Helplessly aware that she wasn't making much sense, Alyssa lifted pained eyes to meet his.

Jordan was grinning with unreserved masculine appreciation. "And the gown sort of went with the casino," he concluded helpfully. "Don't worry, honey, they're perfect on you tonight. Even if you never intended anyone else to see them." He pulled her back into his arms, finding the back clasp of the tiny bra.

"Yes, well, that's just it, you see. I *didn't* intend anyone to see them, and they're rather like this bedroom. A little embarrassing to explain to strangers."

"But we're not strangers, are we, Alyssa?" he countered deeply, the humor fading back into passion. "You and I are kindred souls. I think we already know each other better than most people ever get to know one another, and by morning…" He paused as he slipped the little bra off and bared the soft, full curves of her breasts. "By morning, we will know each other very, very well."

Alyssa's lashes fluttered shut, and she heard herself make the tiniest of kitten cries as Jordan's ultrasensitive fingertips went to her nipples. Trustingly, she once again lifted her arms to encircle his neck and let him find her mouth with his own. She clung to the warmth that flowed between them, trembling again and again in wonder at the passion being generated. When a part of her rational mind tried to interrupt, questioning this complete giving of herself to a man she barely knew, Alyssa pushed the shred of common sense aside. Somehow tonight everything seemed right: the man, the mood, the fantasy. Time enough later to go back to being the real Alyssa Chandler. The odds were against her ever knowing anything quite like this again, and she couldn't bring herself to refuse the promised ecstasy.

He was using the tips of his fingers to draw little circles of fire around each nipple, persuading the budding peaks into an aching, taut fullness that insisted on more and more attention. Alyssa moaned softy and tried to press herself into his hand. Instinctively, her hands began fumbling with the evening jacket he still wore.

"Yes, please," Jordan begged throatily. "Please undress me, sweetheart. Touch me. Hold me. God! I've been wanting you for *hours*."

Without question, Alyssa obeyed, her hands unsteady as she pushed off the charcoal jacket and un-fastened the black studs of the white shirt. All the while, her work was made increasingly difficult as her body continued to respond to Jordan's touch.

When at last she had slipped off his shirt and freed the broad expanse of his chest to her own questing fingers, Alyssa drew in a deep breath of desire.

"Oh, Jordan..." Her fingers entwined themselves eagerly in the curling mat of brown hair that covered his chest, and she probed the flat male nipples in curious wonder. "You're perfect. So perfect."

He managed a husky growl of a laugh, his thumbs grazing lightly across the tips of her breasts as he slid his hands around to her back. "That's supposed to be my line, sweetheart! You're the one who's perfect. A bit of real magic in a world that's full of the fake kind. Perfect."

His hands traveled slowly down the length of her slender back as he pressed her nakedness close against his chest. When her breasts came in contact with the teasing, rasping hair, Jordan moved her very gently back and forth in a swaying motion that made her nipples slide across the crisp, dark cloud. The unexpected caress sent ripples of excitement cascading through Alyssa's veins.

"Jordan, what are you doing to me?" she demanded helplessly, her head tipped back so that she could lose herself in the inviting gold of his eyes.

"It's called sleight of hand," he murmured thickly as his fingers slipped to the upper edge of the tiny black silk panties. "Now you see them"—he peeled the sexy underwear down over the curve of her hip and let it drop to the floor at her ankles—"now you don't. But now I see you. All of you!"

She felt his palms cupping the rounded globes of her buttocks and belatedly remembered the mirrors behind her. He was watching the full length of her body revealed in the mirror, and the knowledge of his blatant hunger sent another rush of heat through her.

"You're not playing fair," she protested shakily, burying her warm face against his broad shoulder.

"There's nothing fair about good sleight of hand,"

he murmured, sinking his nails into the soft flesh of her hips. "It's all magic."

"What do you know of magic?"

"I know a hell of a lot of card tricks," Jordan confessed dryly, and then moved a couple of paces, pulling her with him. "But if it makes you feel any better, we'll even up this situation. There, now you can see as much of me as I can see of you. It's not my fault I'm still half dressed," he added with gentle encouragement. He dropped a soundless kiss in her hair.

Automatically, Alyssa glanced at their figures as they both stood sideways to the wall of mirrors. The sight of herself standing fully naked in the arms of a man who by all of the normal definitions was still a stranger made her gasp. There was something unbearably abandoned about the image, and Alyssa went suddenly still as the realization of what she was doing came home to her. She stared at the image of herself, seeing the way the darker shade of Jordan's skin contrasted with her own paleness, absorbing the possessive curve of his sinewy arms as they encircled her waist. Her bare thighs were arched against his lower body in a silent plea, and even as she watched, momentarily shocked, Jordan deliberately thrust a foot between her legs.

The action, an unsubtle masculine assertion of intent, broke the spell of the mirror. Eyes wide now with an uncertainty that had been sparked far too late,

Alyssa faced him. "Jordan, wait, please wait. This is all happening much too fast, and I can't seem to think. This isn't what I had planned…"

"This isn't what either of us had planned for this evening." The rich, dark voice was a soothing, gentling force designed to ease her rush of indecision. "But it's what's going to happen. I told you earlier that there really is an element of luck in the universe, sweetheart. Don't fight it. I'm not going to *let* you fight it!"

"No, Jordan, wait." She moved her head restlessly from side to side in a negative gesture, but he caught her lips with his own and held them fiercely captive. Then he shifted one hand to burrow it beneath the fall of her auburn hair and find the delicate nape of her neck. Instantly, his fingers began a slow massaging action that calmed and tamed. Alyssa felt herself succumbing to the magic of his hands and the kiss that anchored her mouth. Her palms, which had lifted to his shoulders in protest, stilled once more, hovering uncertainly on his skin.

"I can't wait, sweetheart. I've been looking for you far too long." Jordan's free hand went to the buckle of his belt, and he finished undressing himself impatiently. The beautifully tailored trousers fell into a heap, followed by close-fitting briefs. Before Alyssa had even begun to rescue herself from the spell of his embrace, he, too, was naked.

She felt the brush of his thigh as he thrust it boldly

between hers, parting her legs for his touch. "Jordan, ah, Jordan." The words were a sigh of surrender as he slid his palm across her hip and then began to explore the hidden secrets behind the triangle of auburn hair at the apex of her legs.

"Sweetheart, you're so warm, so ready for me," he groaned as he discovered the evidence of her desire. "Don't deny me what I need so much from you tonight. Stop worrying about the future and go back to thinking only of the present. I'll take care of the future."

Alyssa accepted the fact that she could no longer think properly at all. Her moment of doubt inspired by common sense had passed with the renewed touch of his hand, and she shuddered against him. How could she deny the magic of those hands? Never had she felt anything like it.

She could feel the hardness of his aroused manhood pressing insistently against her hip now, felt the rigidity of his body as the passion in him swelled. Her own body responded with a deep, quivering longing that shocked her senses.

"You see how perfectly we mesh?" Jordan asked whimsically, nudging her head with his hand until Alyssa was once more obliged to glance into the mirrors. She lowered her eyes from the sight of herself entwined so closely in his embrace, but this time she was forced to admit that it hadn't elicited uncertainty.

Rather, she felt another wave of excitement wash across her. Her nails curled of their own volition into the skin of his shoulders, and when she turned her face back against his chest, her teeth nipped daringly.

Jordan groaned and slipped his hands down to her buttocks, letting his fingers slide erotically into the cleft between them. "Whoever shuffled the deck tonight knew what he was doing. Everything's coming up aces."

Alyssa gasped aloud as he used his sensuous hold to lift her a few inches off the floor and force her against the bold demand of his hips. Then her head spun as he carried her that way across the room and set her down onto the red velvet bed.

When she opened her eyes again, Alyssa found herself once more gazing at the sight of her naked body reflected in a mirror, this time the circular one lining the overhead canopy.

"Oh, no!"

Seeing the direction of her gaze, Jordan looked up and grinned appreciatively. When his eyes found her again, Alyssa knew she was flushing vividly. A blatant male hunger prowled in those eyes, waiting to satisfy itself. But that was only fair, she thought suddenly. It had a feminine counterpart deep in the core of her. She wanted this man in a way she had never known before. Wordlessly, she held open her arms.

"Alyssa!" He came down to her quickly, gathering her to him. "I want you so!"

Alyssa forgot about the canopy mirror, forgot about the garish room and the circular bed. She forgot she was with a man she had met only a few hours earlier and about whom she knew almost nothing except that when it came to math, his mind worked rather like her own. All that mattered was that he wanted her and had made her want him with a passion that matched his. The future was forgotten as she played the hand fate had dealt her.

Her body gloried beneath the caresses he administered, shivering and twisting and curling in response. Never would she forget his hands, she thought vaguely as he stroked a line of fire up the inside of her thigh. Wonderful, exquisitely aware fingers, full of strength and power, totally unlike those of any other man in the world, she was certain.

Anxious to please and satisfy in turn, Alyssa explored the contours of his back with her palms, loving the hard feel of him. The muscular planes of his buttocks knew the punishment of her nails, and Jordan groaned beneath it. Pushing her firmly onto her back, he found the taut peak of one breast with his tongue and lips.

Again and again, Alyssa moaned beneath his touch. He trailed tantalizing patterns along every inch of her body from ankle to throat and used his knee to open her legs. Lying half over her in a heavy, passionate sprawl, he whispered incredibly erotic words, words that should have shocked but only served to heighten her own need.

"Now, Jordan, please, now!" She lifted her hips, inviting him into her as, head tipped back across his cradling arm, she squeezed her eyes tightly shut and begged for him.

He caught one of her wrists, urging her hand down his flat stomach to the waiting hardness of him. "Take me, sweetheart. Take me in your soft hand and lead me."

She knew what he was asking; no, demanding. He wanted her to somehow acknowledge that she was a willing player in this dangerous game. Jordan was insisting now that she participate to the fullest. Was he also asking for reassurance? Some final proof that she was as eager and receptive as her body implied?

Whatever the reasons, Alyssa was beyond analyzing them. Her fingers obeyed his husky instructions, thrilling to the feel of him in her hand. Gently, a little timidly, she invited him to follow where she led.

"Oh, God, Alyssa!"

Whatever his intentions, Jordan was unable to play the cards as slowly and tantalizingly as Alyssa sensed he had wanted to do. When her thighs parted, lifting to meet him, he seemed to lose his control. Instead of allowing her to finish her task, he shifted his weight with sudden emphasis, storming her body.

"Sweetheart!"

"Jordan!" His name came in a breathless gasp as he took charge of the hand fate had dealt. He wrapped her tightly against him, surging into her softness and leaving her no option but to respond. Alyssa knew in that moment that although their meeting might have been a matter of chance, Jordan Kyle had no intention of ever letting her forget it. He imprinted his body on hers with all the male power at his command.

He had been every inch the gentleman earlier in the evening, but now there was no gentlemanly attempt to ease the impact of his weight on her body. Jordan made no pretense of using his arms to support himself partially. It was as if he intended she should remember everything about him, including the way his hard frame crushed her luxuriously into the red velvet bedspread.

Her head spinning like a roulette wheel, Alyssa gave herself up completely to the passion of the moment. She clung to the man above her, legs wrapped tightly around his lean hips, her arms around his neck. It was as if Jordan were a dealer who spun the cards out much too fast. There was no opportunity to keep track of them or to figure the odds as the deck was played out. All she could do was accept each new one as it came.

And then she suddenly found herself holding too many cards. There was an unbearable moment of tension, and then the whole pack seemed to explode around her. Her body rippled in Jordan's arms, convulsing in a way that brought a hoarse shout of satisfaction from his own lips. A few seconds later, he was joining her in the release.

Down she tumbled in his arms, dazed and awed at the result of the gamble she had taken. Never had she known anything like this. Never had she known a man who could bring her so fully alive to the bounty of her own senses. For long moments, she lay still, enjoying the feel of his relaxed body lying along hers, knowing a purely feminine satisfaction in having pleased him.

Then she made the mistake of opening her eyes.

"Oh, lord!"

"What's wrong, honey?" Reluctantly, Jordan lifted his head from the comfortable place he had discovered for himself on her breast. Framing her head between his arms he looked down at her, an expression of drowsy contentment in his golden eyes. He used his forefinger to smooth aside a tendril of tangled auburn hair.

"Nothing," she said, grimacing wryly. "Just don't look up."

Her body, lying tangled with his on the red velvet spread, was clearly reflected in the canopy mirror. After one glimpse, Alyssa refused to look up again. In that one glance, she had seen herself as another woman altogether. A sensuous, rather reckless, totally satisfied female lying trapped beneath the hard male body that had brought her such satisfaction. She looked, Alyssa realized belatedly, exactly as a mysterious lady gambler *would* look after meeting her equally mysterious male counterpart.

It was just that she had never really expected to find a counterpart. It had all been intended as fantasy. An amusing way to spend a weekend and make some easy money. What in the world had happened to her?

Jordan's mouth crooked in a wickedly amused smile. "I have no desire to look up. The sight of my own backside doesn't particularly intrigue me, and as far as you're concerned, I prefer the view from down here. Much closer." He feathered a light kiss on her temple and another on her throat. "And the truth is, honey, you look very good lying here beneath me. Perfect, in fact."

Alyssa braved another glimpse in the mirror overhead. "Actually, your backside is a little more intriguing than you might think." She pinched him in an experimental fashion.

"Ouch! If that's the way you're going to show your appreciation, I'm going to deny you the view!"

He rolled to one side, pulling her with him. With a deft movement, Jordan shoved the red velvet bedspread to the carpet, revealing gold sheets. Deftly, he tucked her underneath and followed. When she glanced up at their image in the canopy mirror, it was to see herself modestly swathed to the throat in a sheet. Alyssa glanced around the red plush room and started to smile. A pleasantly dazed, languid sensation was protecting her now from reality.

"What's so funny?" Jordan demanded easily, folding his arms behind his head and watching her.

"I just realized. The Porsche that I'm going to buy— It's almost the same shade of red as this room! I think when I finally get ready to place the order, I might change the color."

"No, don't do that." He reached for her, tugging her across his chest. His golden eyes gleamed very brilliantly. "Get the red one. That way, whenever you drive it, you'll think of this night and this room."

The laughter went out of her in the face of his intensity. Abruptly, the truth of what he was saying made itself felt. But she had no need to buy a red car in order to make herself remember what had happened this weekend. Alyssa knew she would never forget this night, this room or this man.

That realization brought with it another: no matter what happened this weekend, she must be certain that no one in her real world ever discovered the fantasy she had created for herself. The lifestyle and the career she valued so much would be put in jeopardy if the truth were ever known.

Jordan must have seen the flicker of wariness that came and went in her sea-colored eyes because abruptly he cradled her face between his hands and pulled her close for a warm, lingering kiss. She felt his body hardening under hers and lifted her lashes to gaze down at him wonderingly.

"Jordan?"

His eyes laughed up at her with the promise of renewed passion. "I said the sight of my own backside in that mirror didn't particularly intrigue me. Yours, however, is another matter."

"Jordan!"

But he had already thrown the sheet off her and was guiding her body astride his. His warm, strong hands gently circled her waist, urging her to him completely, and as she obeyed, Alyssa forgot about the overhead mirror, the red Porsche and the threat to her career that this weekend represented.

She gave herself up again to the fantasy and the man who had brought it to life.

CHAPTER THREE

THE FIRST THING ALYSSA SAW THE NEXT morning when she opened her eyes was Jordan Kyle calmly going through her purse. He was standing unabashedly naked beside the low table where she had thoughtlessly dropped the sequined mesh evening bag the night before. The money she had won was neatly stacked on the table, and he was flipping interestedly through the calfskin wallet when he noticed she was awake.

"Good morning, Alyssa Meredith Chandler of Ventura, California. And happy belated birthday." Jordan glanced back down at the date on her driver's license. "Let's see, you turned thirty last week, didn't you?"

Alyssa lay very still beneath the gold sheet, her eyes never leaving the face of the stranger who had become her lover. Dear God, what had happened to her? How could she have been so incredibly stupid? Was she about to become the victim of a professional thief who made a practice of seducing women who had won at the tables and then robbing them? The thoughts flickered through her mind as her hand tightened on the sheet at her throat.

Jordan glanced up again from the driver's license, and his gaze narrowed as he took in the stark, uncomprehending expression on Alyssa's features. Her auburn hair was tangled from where he had run his hands through it during the night, and her mouth had a vulnerable, almost-bruised fullness about it. The sea-green eyes were wide and cautious, holding no sign of the hidden laughter that normally lurked just below the surface. There was a faintly reddened area on the soft skin of her throat, and the sight of it elicited a short, disgusted oath.

"Hell, I should have remembered to shave before taking you to bed last night." He raised a hand to the shadow of an incipient beard on his jaw and simultaneously tossed the wallet down beside the money. "I'm afraid I've marked you, sweetheart. My only excuse is that I wasn't thinking very clearly by the time I got you back to the room!"

Alyssa watched him warily as he came toward her. He seemed very much a lean, male animal in the morning sunlight. Without the sophisticated veneer of his evening clothes, there was little trace of last night's gentleman gambler about Jordan Kyle this morning. The fear that had awakened in her a few minutes before when she'd opened her eyes to find him systematically going through her purse went up another notch. Her body was a slender, taut length outlined by the gold sheet.

"Alyssa Meredith Chandler. Age thirty and a couple of days. Resides in Ventura, California, and works as a statistician for a company called Yeoman Research." Jordan repeated what he had learned about her as if savoring each small fact. He leaned down as he reached the bed, planting a palm on either side of her body to form a cage with his arms, trapping her. "And unmarried. Thank God." The golden eyes burned over her tense face.

"Do you always go through a woman's purse the morning after?" Alyssa muttered, trying for some semblance of bravado. A semblance was all it was. She didn't feel particularly brave lying there with him looming over her like some vengeful devil. Yes, devil. Hadn't they once called casinos "gambling hells"? And with those golden eyes and those hands... Her body heated uncomfortably at the memory of those hands on it.

"Last night," Jordan told her carefully, "I wanted you too badly to risk asking too many questions. This morning, when I woke up, I realized just how little I knew about you. It occurred to me, in fact, that you might even be married. I had to get some answers, honey, and I wasn't too sure you'd be willing to part with them. That didn't leave me much choice. But you're not married, are you?"

"Would it matter?"

"Are you?" This time the question was dangerous.

"No. Not anymore," she whispered starkly. "Are you?"

"No. We're a little late with some of the more pertinent questions, aren't we? But I suppose better late than never."

A sense of indignation began to eat away at the uncertain fear he had inspired in her. "Can I assume from the tone of this inquisition that you really are just curious about me? You're not planning to take my money and disappear?"

One dark brow lifted deliberately. "Is that what you thought I was doing when you woke up? Getting ready to steal last night's winnings?"

"The thought crossed my mind." Alyssa struggled up onto one elbow, but he didn't remove his caging arms. The lean power in his nude body seemed to be reaching out to suffocate her. She felt trapped, and she was far too aware of the strength in him. She should be. Her body still ached from it. "After all, I don't know any more about you than you know about me."

He stared at her broodingly for a long moment. "No. You probably don't. Last night, in the heat of passion, I told myself that once I had you in bed, all the questions would be answered. I thought we'd know each other very well by this morning. And we do in some ways. I just hadn't realized how many questions there would remain to be asked. I seem to have developed an insatiable curiosity about you, Alyssa Meredith Chandler. I want to know everything there is to know, and taking you to bed only gave me some of the answers. My biggest single fear when I opened my eyes and saw you lying there beside me was that I might have been cast in the role of the other man."

"Somehow I don't see you playing that part," she retorted caustically.

"Neither do I," he agreed a little too blandly. "But given the fact that I went to sleep without even learning your last name, it was a distinct possibility."

"You're in a rather negative mood this morning, aren't you?" she observed. "Do I get to go through your wallet now?" It was only a faint sally, and Alyssa was rather surprised when it worked. She hadn't really expected him to free her and walk across the room to fish the elegantly thin leather billfold out of the pocket of his slacks, but he did. She sucked in her breath in temporary relief as his weight left the bed.

Wordlessly, he strode back across the room and dropped the wallet on her lap. Then he lounged at the foot of the bed and waited while she flipped through it.

Feeling awkward at riffling through his personal things but not knowing what else to do now that she had demanded to see them, Alyssa hurriedly flipped through the few items. The driver's license was issued to one Jordan Kyle at an Oregon address. Alyssa automatically calculated his age from the birth date given and came up with thirty-nine. She had been right when she'd suspected he was dangerously near the forty-year mark.

"Hmmm," she noted with an unexpected surge of wry amusement. "No visible means of support. How does a professional get credit cards?" She held up a couple of pieces of the magic plastic.

His mouth curved wryly. "It's not easy. Not at first. Eventually, the bank stops asking questions when one's account becomes sufficiently large."

"I'll have to remember that."

"You don't have that problem. After all, you have a real job. Honest employment. Banks love people like you."

She glanced up, surprised by the curious note in his voice. He looked half intrigued and half wary. The thought crossed her mind very briefly that he seemed almost envious. No, that was crazy. He was the one with the exotic lifestyle, living the fantasy to the hilt. She only dropped in on the illusion occasionally.

"I have the feeling that your bank is probably lots more in love with you than mine is with me. Something tells me your account is considerably more established. After all, I've just started, uh, supplementing mine."

"What do you tell people when you blow your

ill-gotten gains on something frivolous? How will you explain the red Porsche when you buy it?" he asked deliberately.

"If anyone asks, I'll tell him I've had a good year in the stock market," she said uneasily. This wasn't a subject she wanted to pursue.

"Why not tell the truth?" Jordan persisted coolly, his eyes studying her with an intensity that made her even more nervous.

"That would be impossible," she stated flatly. "The truth would cost me my job."

"You're kidding! Cost you your job?"

"Ummm. That company I work for, Yeoman Research? It prides itself on having several government contracts as well as some other business-sensitive research arrangements. People who gamble as much as I've been doing lately are considered something of an employment risk in situations like that, to say the least. We're seen as being particularly vulnerable to blackmail and pressure in order to pay off gambling debts. We might very well resort to selling company secrets, or worse, government ones. If the management at Yeoman Research knew I was spending so much of my time in Las Vegas lately, I would undoubtedly be quietly asked to leave or, at the minimum, transferred to a less sensitive position on the staff. That would be almost as bad from my point of view."

"Why?"

"Because I'm in line for promotion. With luck, I will be named the new manager of my department next month," Alyssa told him, unable to hide her satisfaction at the thought. "I've worked hard, and I deserve the slot. I like the statistical research and analysis I do."

"Better than you like winning at the card tables?"

"I happen to enjoy both," she said very steadily, "and I don't see why I can't have both." If I'm very careful, she amended silently.

"That's known as having your cake and eating it, too, and as I recall, it doesn't always work," Jordan pointed out politely.

"I'm going to make it work." Alyssa tossed his wallet back at him. Jordan caught it almost absently. Excellent eye-hand coordination, she decided with a sigh. Gained after years of experience at his profession, no doubt. "Now, if we've quite finished with the interrogation this morning, I'd like to get dressed and go back to my hotel room." Might as well try to salvage what dignity there was left in this situation, she told herself forcefully. It would have been easier if he weren't lying naked at the end of the round bed.

"You can't leave yet," Jordan informed her gently.

"Why not?" Alyssa lifted her chin challengingly.

"You haven't seen how the shower works in that tacky bathroom." Quite suddenly, he was grinning again. The engaging, piratical grin that she'd only caught flashes of last night. To her shock, Alyssa realized she was coming to like that grin very, very much.

"I was getting the impression you were a little annoyed with me this morning," she said carefully. "I thought it might be best to be on my way."

The golden eyes gleamed. "I think I was more annoyed with myself than I was with you," he admitted. "I woke up with too many questions and too many worries. Bound to make a man grouchy in the morning. But don't get the idea that I'm going to throw you out. That's the last thing I plan to do!"

Alyssa wasn't sure whether to be relieved or more wary than ever. She sat up slowly, holding the sheet in place at her throat and drawing up her knees in front of her. "Were you really worried when you woke up?"

"Is it so strange that I'd at least like to know the last name of the woman with whom I spent the night?" he countered, eyeing her laconically.

Alyssa felt the flush rise to her cheekbones, but she kept her gaze very steady. "I was under the impression that here in Vegas such details weren't considered very important. Last night, you didn't seem overly concerned."

"Last night, I told myself nothing else mattered except getting you into bed and staking a claim on you," he retorted with a bluntness that deepened the red in her cheeks. "I wanted you from the first instant I saw you winning so coolly and deliberately. I decided you had probably been made just for me. A soul mate and lover."

"Jordan…"

"But getting you into bed didn't solve all the problems. As thoroughly satisfying as the experience was, it seems to have left me very, very hungry for more answers. It also left me exceedingly nervous. If there's one thing I can't afford to be in my profession, it's nervous. Plays havoc with my concentration."

"I see," she grumbled aloofly.

Without any warning, he launched himself toward her, pushing her back down into the bedclothes and pinning her beneath him. "I doubt that you do see, little lady gambler. Do you have any idea what it does to a man to wake up wondering if he's playing the part of the other man? If there's a husband waiting patiently in the wings back in Ventura?"

Violently aware of the warmth of his body through the sheet, Alyssa stared up at him wonderingly, beginning to lose herself in the depths of those golden eyes, just as she had last night. "Why was it so important that you find out if I'm married?" she dared, waiting breathlessly for his answer.

"Because I don't want to be the other man. I want to be the *only* man in your life now that I've found you." Jordan emphasized the uncompromising word with a quick, hard kiss as if he were branding her. "Having gone through your wallet, I'm reasonably certain there's no husband hanging about, though."

"And if there had been?"

"Professional gamblers don't worry about nonexistent probabilities," he declared softly. "There are always enough of the real kind around. Which brings us to the next item on the list. There's no husband back in Ventura, but is there anyone else who thinks he has a claim on you?"

"So many questions," she whispered uncomprehendingly. Men who casually picked up lone women and seduced them were reputed to be just as casual about walking away from them the next morning. Jordan was behaving like a possessive lover who intended to stick around.

"You have the easy part. All you have to do is answer the questions."

"Asking them is the hard part?"

"Not knowing all the answers is the hard part," he corrected smoothly. "Don't keep me in suspense, honey. Is there anyone waiting for you back in Ventura? Not that I can imagine any man in his right mind allowing you to traipse off to Vegas by yourself!"

"I'm thirty years old. I stopped asking other people's permission to do things a long time ago!"

"I'll bet you did." He grinned suddenly. "A man

would have his work cut out for him training you to start asking again, wouldn't he?"

"Damn right," she muttered, hovering between excitement and annoyance. She had never met a man like Jordan Kyle, and the magic of last night was persisting. She couldn't seem to shake his spell. "Would you mind if we continued this interrogation after breakfast? I'm hungry."

"I'll feed you after you answer my question," he growled softly.

"Jordan," she sighed, "I can't see that any of your questions matter very much. We've only known each other a few hours, and after this weekend, we'll never see each other again." Alyssa found herself defensively wanting to be the first to put the truth into words. "But since I'm hungry and since you're a lot heavier than I am, I will tell you that at the moment my social life is very casual, to say the least. No, there is no one who will wonder where I am this weekend and worry about it."

He studied her carefully for several seconds and then nodded once in satisfaction. "Okay, that much is settled. I guess we can get ready to go have breakfast. Come and see the tacky shower."

He started to lever himself up off her body, and without pausing to think about it, Alyssa put out a hand and touched his bare shoulder. He turned back to her at once. "What about you?" she heard herself ask, her voice sounding strained. Suddenly, it was she who had to have some answers.

Jordan tilted his head thoughtfully, a smile appearing on his mouth. "I was beginning to think you didn't care enough yet to inquire. No, sweetheart, there's no one else. Professional gamblers seldom acquire much in the way of family or permanent women."

She caught her breath. "Well, that's honest enough, at least." This really was going to turn out to be a one-weekend affair. But, then, she'd realized that from the beginning, hadn't she? Summoning up an incredible amount of bravado, she managed a smile. "If you're sure you're not going to abscond with my winnings from last night, I suppose you might as well let me at the tacky bathroom."

He grinned, looking suddenly like a man who is quite happy and somewhat surprised to find himself in that state. Alyssa wondered how much happiness and contentment was generally allotted to professional gamblers. As a fantasy, the gambling world was exciting and intriguing, fascinating to drop in on now and then. But as a way of life?

"That must have been something of a shock, waking up to find me going through your wallet." He ducked his head and kissed her lightly on the forehead. "I'm sorry, honey. To make up for it, I'll do more than let you at the tacky bathroom. I'll help you take your shower."

"Thanks! Talk about tacky!"

But it was too late to complain. He had already whipped back the gold sheet and reached down to lift her into his arms. Alyssa yelped in protest, but he ignored her, striding across the red carpet to the red and gold bathroom, which was another hall of mirrors. Alyssa had had a brief glimpse last night of the small figures of naked women from which the water flowed in the sink. She had also noted the oversized shower, which had obviously been designed for two people and came complete with seats. She had the distinct impression that turning Jordan loose in the exotic room in his present mood was just asking for trouble.

She was right. It was another hour before they went down to breakfast.

"I'd have ordered room service, but it tends to be rather slow in these huge hotels," Jordan explained cheerfully as they finally sat down to eat in the twenty-four-hour coffee shop. "And I'm starving."

"I'd have thought they would have things like room service down to a fine art," Alyssa observed, sipping gratefully at a cup of tea.

"That's just it; they do have it down to an art here in Vegas." Jordan chuckled, glancing at his menu. "They're well aware of the fact that slow room service drives people downstairs to get something to eat or drink."

"Ah, I get it. And once downstairs, they have to walk through the casino to get to a restaurant or a bar."

"Exactly. You can't get anywhere in this hotel or any of the other big ones without going through the casino. A fine art."

Even at this early hour, the tinkle of slot machines out on the gambling floor was audible. Some of the card tables were closed, but several were in use, and a dedicated crowd of gamblers had obviously made an early start on the day. Or perhaps they had never gone to bed last night, Alyssa decided. With a wry smile, she glanced down at the black and silver dress she'd been forced to put on this morning.

"I've got to get back to my hotel. I look like one of those seedy gamblers who never made it home last night," she groaned.

Casual in a cotton button-down-collar shirt done in a conservative pin stripe and a pair of khaki chinos, Jordan didn't look at all seedy, she had decided earlier as she covertly watched him dress. His dark hair was clean and damp from the shower, and there was an easy, relaxed air about him this morning that belied his profession. Sitting across from him in her evening gown, Alyssa felt very much a lady of the night who hadn't made it back to her own bed. Which was, she reminded herself grimly, exactly the case.

"Stop worrying about how you look," Jordan advised dryly. "No one will even notice here."

But he caught a cab for them back to her hotel after breakfast, anyway, because, he said, he wanted her to get a swim suit. "I thought we could spend the afternoon by the pool," he explained as they rode the elevator up to her room. "Have to gather our energy so we can go to work tonight. I figure with both of us on the job, you'll have your thousand bucks by around midnight, and then we can knock off and take in one of the big lounge shows."

Alyssa froze, her key in the lock of the door. "What do you mean, 'both of us on the job'? Jordan, I don't need your help in getting the money for my Porsche." Somehow she wanted to make that very clear.

His smile faded as he took in the stubborn expression in her eyes. "I know you don't *need* my help, but it will speed things up considerably if you let me give you a hand."

It was true, of course. Alyssa made it a rule to keep all of her wins on a small scale in order to avoid suspicion. Working alone, it would take most of that night and Sunday to gather the thousand dollars. With Jordan's help, it could be done in a much shorter time. But the thought of taking money from him after spending the weekend in his bed went against her grain.

"No, Jordan. Please. I don't want any help." She twisted the key violently in the lock and pushed at the door, not looking at him.

He caught her shoulder as she stepped into the room, spinning her around to face him as the door clicked shut behind them. His tawny eyes blazed down at her, all trace of his easy, relaxed mood gone. The infinitely skilled fingers proved as knowledgeable in the art of subtle punishment as they were in dealing cards or giving pleasure. He didn't quite hurt her, but Alyssa found herself not daring to move. It crossed her mind that Jordan Kyle would be a very dangerous man under certain circumstances.

"Alyssa, I'm not trying to pay you for this weekend," he said bluntly.

She drew in a breath. "That's what it would seem like you were doing," she said carefully.

"That's ridiculous."

"Is it?"

"You know damn well it is!" he retorted.

"I hardly know you at all, Jordan. That's just the point," Alyssa said with unnatural calm. "And I'd rather not take money from you. Let me rephrase that. I *won't* take money from you. Do I make myself very clear?"

The fingers on her bare shoulder dug a little deeper, and the hard lines of his face seemed to have been etched in steel. "Oh, yes. You make yourself very clear. It's quite *clear* that you're being stubborn, illogical and overly sensitive, but if you insist on behaving like that—"

"I do."

"Then I'll let you get away with it. For a while." He

freed her shoulder with an obvious effort at self-control and glanced around the hotel room. "Now why don't you change your clothes so that we can stop wasting the day."

Hiding a sigh of relief, Alyssa obeyed. She felt as if she'd had a rather narrow escape, although she wasn't precisely sure what she had avoided.

Her weekend Las Vegas wardrobe included a sleek, strapless maillot diagonally striped in black and white and piped at the upper edge in crimson. Over it, she wore an overscaled white cotton cover-up that she had bought a week earlier. Styled with push-up sleeves and a red sash, it fell to her knees and doubled as a casual dress. When she reappeared from the bathroom, Jordan's eyes flickered with approval, and he inclined his head in a gravely polite manner.

"Does anyone back in Venture know the real you?" he asked whimsically.

"No one knows how I've been spending my weekends lately, if that's what you mean," she admitted. And what a disaster it would be if anyone did!

"Not exactly, but we'll let it pass for now. Come on, my sweet business associate. Let's go find a pool and prepare ourselves for a hard night's work."

That evening, after dinner, when Alyssa walked into the first casino on Jordan's arm, she did so with a whole new appreciation for the fantasy. It was infinitely more enjoyable sharing it with a man who truly belonged to this world, she decided.

"Do you ever feel like a marauding shark swimming through a casino and taking a bite here and there?" Alyssa demanded laughingly as she joined Jordan after he'd walked out of a poker game with a discreet pile of chips.

He looked down at her and smiled faintly. "Sometimes. How are you doing?"

"Okay. I'm going to play a little more blackjack and then quit for the evening."

"I've made enough tonight to put you over the top of your goal," he reminded her quietly.

"I'm on schedule," she retorted firmly.

"All right. Have it your way. I don't want you lying in my arms tonight thinking I've somehow paid you to be there!" Jordan muttered half violently.

She slid a slanting glance up at his set face and decided not to say anything further on the subject. She had won the small battle, and that was enough for now.

He watched her play with silent approval, and Alyssa found herself enjoying the admiration of a peer. It was a novel experience, and when she picked up her chips and walked away from the blackjack table, she was feeing deliciously contented.

They caught the midnight cabaret in the show room of Jordan's hotel, and afterward he led her into a nearby lounge for a nightcap. The evening had been perfect as far as Alyssa was concerned, and he must have seen the pleasure in her eyes.

"To the only woman I've ever met with whom I can truly discuss my work," he saluted her, smiling as he took a sip of the brandy he had ordered for both of them. Then he set down the snifter and asked evenly, "You'll be coming back to Vegas next weekend, of course?"

A strange tension gripped her as Alyssa faced him across the small table. She hadn't been expecting the question. Her mind had been on the present, just as it had been the night before. For a woman who made a living using statistics to predict future events, she had been doing a remarkably good job of ignoring her own future.

"Why do you say, of course?" she countered as lightly as possible.

"Because at the conservative rate you're working, you've got quite a way to go before you have the down payment on that red Porsche. Vegas is the closest source of easy money for you, so I assumed you'd be coming here rather regularly for a while. Right?" He leaned back casually in his chair, his eyes never leaving her face. She felt as if she were a deck of cards he had shuffled and was now about to play with. It was not a comfortable sensation.

"Well, yes, I had planned on returning soon," she agreed hesitantly.

"Don't bother with hotel reservations," he said politely. "You'll be staying with me."

She held her breath. Part of her wanted to give way to the thrill of happiness that accompanied the notion of seeing him again the following weekend. But another part of her advised caution. The whole situation was so unreal, so much a fantasy for her, that she couldn't analyze it properly. That knowledge alone should inspire a great deal of care, she told herself.

"You're going to be here next weekend?" she hedged.

"I'll be here for at least another couple of weeks. Then I'll be going to Oregon."

"Your home?"

"As much of a home as I've got, yes," he agreed dismissively. "When will you be arriving? Friday night? I'll pick you up at the airport."

He was rushing her, crowding her into agreement, not giving her a chance to think. She knew what he was doing and had a hunch he did, too. The catch was that she wanted to be hurried along. The lure of spending another fantasy weekend with this man was almost irresistible.

"Do you really want me to spend another weekend with you?" she whispered, her eyes shining.

"You know the answer to that. I want you, Alyssa. I've never tried to make a secret of that fact. What about you? Do you want the time with me?"

Alyssa was unable to hold the golden eyes. Her own gaze dropped to the snifter in her hand as she whispered the truth. "Yes."

"Then we'll make your flight reservations tomorrow when I take you to the airport. Next Friday evening, I'll be waiting for you." There was a note of fierce satisfaction in his dark voice.

"Same room?" Alyssa found the courage to tease him.

"I'll see if I can find another one even more interesting to surprise you with," he promised.

"Oh, no! The one you have is quite surprising enough, thanks!"

"Then why don't we go on upstairs and discover whatever else it has to offer?" he suggested deliberately, setting down his glass with an air of finality and getting to his feet.

She sensed the male decision in him. He was more than ready to carry her off to bed, and wrapped as she was in the magic of the illusion, Alyssa could not have protested if she had wanted to do so. Obediently, she allowed him to take her arm and guide her out of the cocktail lounge.

They walked past the roped-off baccarat table where elegantly attired men and women lost their money to a croupier in a tuxedo, and Jordan smiled.

"One thing you get for your money at baccarat is a classy environment," he observed.

"That's about all you get. With the rules so completely established by the house, I have yet to figure out a way to better the odds in that game," Alyssa said sadly.

Jordan shrugged. "I doubt that anyone has. Theoretically, the house edge is only a little over one percent in baccarat, but there isn't any room for skill or mathematics, and people lose quite steadily. It holds no appeal for real gamblers or people like you and me, but that doesn't seem to stop a lot of folks from wanting to play."

"It's because of the image," Alyssa decided wisely. "What with everyone having to dress to the hilt to play and the croupier and the ladderman in tuxes and the whole area cordoned off, it makes one feel elegantly European and rich. The illusion is everything in gambling."

Jordan glanced down at her. "So it is. But you and I see past the illusion, don't we? Our magic is possible because we see the mathematical structure behind the façade and we have a feel for it."

"Yes, I suppose so." They were in the elevator now, and Alyssa shivered at the inevitable approach of passion. They were talking of math and probabilities and gambling, and all she could think about was what it would be like in a few minutes when Jordan took her in his arms. It was a dizzying, reckless sensation that made it difficult to think with anything remotely resembling her usual logic.

When they stepped out into the corridor that led to

the bordello-red bedroom, Alyssa swayed slightly, and when Jordan's arm immediately came around her, she leaned gratefully into his strength. Amazing, she thought contentedly.

"What's amazing?" Jordan asked, opening the door to his room.

Alyssa blinked up at him, unaware she had spoken aloud. "You are," she explained politely as he led her inside.

"And why is that?" His smile was one of anticipation and passion and gentleness as he pulled her close. The golden eyes seemed to go molten, and Alyssa thought she would melt under the heat of them.

"Because you're so strong, so solid, so real," she heard herself whisper as she lifted her arms to encircle his neck. "Illusions aren't supposed to be so very real."

Her lashes had fluttered shut as she raised her mouth for his kiss, and so she did not see the hardness that appeared in the depths of his gaze. "Alyssa," Jordan growled softly as he picked her up and carried her over to the round bed, bathed in desert moonlight, "don't ever make the mistake of thinking I'm not quite real. Don't put me in the category of illusion, honey, or you will find yourself taking what will undoubtedly be the first genuine gamble of your life. And I guarantee you will lose." ·

But Alyssa was too wrapped up in this new world of sensation to heed the warning.

CHAPTER FOUR

THE JET HEADING BACK TO LOS ANGELES International had just reached fifteen thousand feet when Alyssa remembered the dinner party she was scheduled to give the following Friday evening.

With that memory, reality came flooding back. Instinctively, she turned in the seat, straining to glance back in the direction of Las Vegas, but the glittering city in the middle of the desert was already out of sight. Jordan would have caught a cab back to his hotel. In another couple of hours, he would be preparing to go to work. The night shift, she decided in wry humor. Her lover worked the night shift at his job. And when she was with him, she had done the same.

But real life was a respectable position with a sophisticated research and testing firm. Working the night shift in Vegas was a weekend illusion, a dangerous fantasy that had somehow become incredibly alive during the past couple of days. Alyssa turned back in her seat, staring blindly at the magazine in her lap. She had allowed herself to be utterly and completely seduced by her fantasy this weekend.

Never in her life had she succumbed so totally to the spell of a man. Never had she been the type to become involved in weekend flings or one-night stands. The knowledge that she had done exactly that during the past couple of days left her feeling dazed and a little out of control of herself. This wasn't a side of herself that she knew or understood. She lowered her lashes uneasily as she contemplated the unsettling facts.

Even though she had gone over some invisible edge this weekend, she had only herself to blame. Hadn't she been dancing closer and closer to the precipice each time she'd gone to Las Vegas during the past few months?

No, damn it, she hadn't been in this kind of danger until this past weekend, she corrected herself forcefully. There had never been a man involved in her fantasy. There had been no temptation or seduction of that sort whatsoever. Not until she had encountered Jordan Kyle.

And Jordan Kyle was unlike any other man she had ever met.

Since that disastrous year of her marriage to Chad Emerson, Alyssa knew she had found it relatively easy to keep from becoming entangled in any truly serious emotional commitment. She'd had enough to do proving herself in the business world. But humiliation at her own stupidity still surged to the surface occasionally when she thought about that painful year and a half after her graduation from college.

Her father had done his best to raise her, she realized. But he'd been so hoping for a mathematical prodigy to more or less take his place in the upper reaches of the academic research world that he'd firmly guided his daughter into math. Alyssa hadn't minded. She loved the subject and had a flair for it. But having a flair was not the same as having a true genius for it. Reluctantly, because she longed to please her father, she'd focused more and more on applied mathematics rather than pure mathematics.

Applied math was the kind that was needed on a day-to-day basis in the working world. From her end of the spectrum came the statisticians, the engineering mathematicians, the *practical* math people, without whom all the work of the geniuses such as her father would have been wasted. People in applied math were the ones who took the brilliant discoveries and techniques and turned them to useful purposes in the areas of accounting, computers, engineering, insurance and a thousand other fields. The geniuses wound up teaching and conducting research at the finest universities in the country.

She knew her father had been vastly disappointed when it became evident that she wasn't going to follow precisely in his footsteps, and it hurt Alyssa to know she had failed him. But in her senior year of college, she thought she had found a way to pacify him. That was when Chad Emerson had first started paying attention to her.

From a very practical point of view, it was often far easier for a graduate in applied math to get a paying job right out of college than for one with a more theoretical background. Chad Emerson, for all his brilliance, apparently had had a very down to earth grasp of that basic fact. He'd also fully appreciated the unquestioned eminence of the man who was her father. Joseph Chandler could be a tremendous asset as a father-in-law. He held an important post at a fine university. Chad had wanted to assure himself of not only getting into the right graduate school but of making the right contacts. Being brilliant was great, but politics always helped.

Alyssa had gone along willingly with the whirlwind courtship Chad had instituted. Her father had been enormously pleased after meeting the young man she proposed to marry. If his daughter wasn't quite smart enough to take a place in the stellar list of brilliant mathematicians, she was smart enough to marry someone who eventually would. Knowing she had pleased her father and flattered by the overwhelming attention of a fellow student whom she had admired from afar, Alyssa had agreed to Chad's proposal of marriage.

It occurred to Alyssa on occasion that she'd never really set her own goals. For years, her father had established them for her, and later, married to Chad and working to pay his graduate student fees, she had attempted to gain her satisfaction through helping her husband attain his lofty goals. And there *was* some satisfaction along that route. Being with Chad, entertaining his brilliant friends, gave her a sense of participating in the elite world of mathematicians, a world she'd always been taught to respect.

For a time, Chad had seemed content with his admiring wife, whose practical ability had won her an excellent paying position right out of college. Joseph Chandler certainly fulfilled his duties as a proud father-in-law, helping his daughter's husband get into the graduate school of his choice and making certain he was brought to the attention of the right people.

But a year and a half after marrying her, Chad was offered a teaching assistant's post at the university. He had been recognized by the people who mattered. Along with the new position came introductions to new people. Perhaps it was inevitable that Chad would eventually meet a woman who was more suited to his intellectual level. In any event, he evidently felt he no longer needed Joseph Chandler's support or a hard-working wife. He had divorced Alyssa to marry a beautiful and unquestionably brilliant faculty member who would undoubtedly take over the furthering of his career.

It had all been for the best, Alyssa had told herself a thousand times since then. She would never have felt entirely comfortable in Chad's environment. There would always have been that feeling of inferiority with which to contend, that knowledge that she could never compete with his brilliant friends. And there was no doubt that from her very humble, very practical point of view, it hadn't been pleasant learning that Chad had basically seen her as a meal ticket and her father as an added asset.

But all the common sense in the world didn't alleviate the feeling of rejection that struck her like a hammer when her former friends, the ones Chad had cultivated, no longer found her particularly interesting. It was Chad's intelligence and upward mobility in the academic world that had drawn them. They had nothing in common with his wife.

And all the common sense in the world couldn't dispel the notion that she'd somehow disappointed her father for not being able to hold on to Chad. She'd brought a brilliant mathematician into the family, a man who could have been a true son to the elder Chandler, only to lose him.

Alyssa's reaction had been abrupt and single-minded. If she wasn't good enough for the academic world, she'd damn well prove she could hold her own in other spheres! Namely, a sphere where her brand of math was appreciated, sought after and paid for. She dedicated herself to the business world, where she had since proved more than able to rise steadily to the top.

In the area of statistics and probability theory, she had shown real flair, and Alyssa was determined to be as successful at her job as Chad and her father were in their worlds. She measured her success by the salary and title she held. They were the only gauges she had. Her father had been accidentally killed in an automobile crash just about the time Alyssa was starting to demonstrate her true abilities. She'd never known for sure whether or not he had really respected her progress in the corporate world. Not knowing had seemed to make it all the more imperative to succeed. She had driven herself relentlessly for the past two years.

Then, a couple of months earlier, because of Ray and Julia Burgess, she had discovered the world of gambling. It had proved a wonderful escape from the self-inflicted pressures under which she worked. What would Chad or her father have said if they had ever learned that her one area of "genius" in the realm of mathematics had proved to be an intuitive ability to play cards and roll dice? She didn't really have to wonder. They would have been thoroughly disgusted.

But the fantasy world of gambling offered her exactly what she had been needing. It freed the cheerful, fun-loving, playful side of her personality. It was when she was in that world that the mischievous smile lit her eyes, and sometimes that smile carried over into her real world when she returned. She needed the escape. She needed to throw herself into the exciting fantasy where her one true talent reigned supreme.

She had known from the beginning, of course, that her "escape" represented a very real threat to her carefully built career. And the goals of that career and its accompanying lifestyle were too much a part of her to even consider abandoning them. The trick, she told herself, was to keep the fantasy world separate from her real world, and she'd been quite successful at managing that feat. Perhaps she even took a certain pleasure in managing it. Even Alyssa wasn't fully aware of the hidden smile that played in her eyes these days when she took on the challenge of juggling her two lives.

The excitement of her new, secret world had put a flare of energy into her life and a subtle recklessness into her way of looking into things. Until this weekend, however, she had thought she had both under full control. Jordan Kyle had taught her differently. He had materialized out of her fantasy and had at once made it far more real and therefore more dangerous than she would have dreamed possible.

What did he really think of her? The world of gambling was still largely a man's world. When women played, for example, it was assumed they played with some man's money. No Las Vegas gentleman would be so ungallant as to allow a woman companion to risk her own money! The attitude toward women in places like Las Vegas and Reno was as traditional and conservative as that of mythical small-town America. Women fit either into the category of showgirl-hustler or wife-mother. A woman who manipulated the world of gambling, who dealt with it on its own terms and won, would have been almost impossible for either the gambling establishment or most men, in general, to understand. And if they did understand, they would have invariably seen her as a threat.

But Jordan Kyle had been the exception. Was that why she had found herself so easily seduced by him? He had admired her ability. Alyssa closed her eyes, trying to sort out her memories of the weekend. There had been an incredible enticement in the knowledge that he had known from the first exactly what she was doing and had fully appreciated her peculiar "talent." When his own talent had proved to run along exactly the same lines, she had been fascinated. Together they were like a pair of mathematical magicians sharing secrets no one else knew.

Added to the intellectual attraction had been a level of passion utterly new to her. Never had she known the sheer, raging excitement she had discovered in the arms of her golden-eyed gambler.

And because of that combination of irresistible

lures, Alyssa knew she wanted to return to Las Vegas the following weekend.

The dinner party on Friday night, however, was important in her other life, her real life. It was important career-wise because she would be entertaining her boss and his wife among others, and it was important socially because she would be seeing friends, maintaining a normal round of activities for herself.

For what she had found in Las Vegas was an alluring illusion that must not be allowed to interfere with the reality of her weekday world. If it did, it would destroy that world. And she had worked so long and so hard…

She sighed, leaning back in the seat and resting her hand protectively on the zipper bag that contained her winnings from the past few days. She would have to phone Jordan and explain that she would not be on the Friday-night flight, after all. But there shouldn't be much problem in booking a Saturday-morning flight, she reassured herself.

Alyssa was exhausted by the time she located her small compact car at the L.A. airport and drove home to Ventura. The pleasant town on the California coast between Los Angeles and Santa Barbara had been home to her now for the past four years, ever since she had accepted the position with Yeoman Research. She had been lucky enough to find a beach-front house to rent. Her present salary was high enough now to allow her to afford the luxury.

Someday that salary would be high enough to allow her to buy the red Porsche, too, she reminded herself wryly as she parked the compact in the garage and slowly climbed out. If she got that promotion, for example, she might be able to make the down payment. But it had proved more interesting to acquire the Porsche with gambling winnings.

The automatic garage door mechanism hissed the door shut behind her as she let herself into the small, neat house through the kitchen entrance. The cottage faced the sea, and on clear days one could see the Channel Islands just off shore.

She had taken full advantage of the view, orienting the furniture around it. The beach-front atmosphere had been maintained with a color scheme of white and yellow and natural woods. Luxuriantly green plants cascaded from ceiling hangers and filled every available corner. Blinds with elegantly thin slats could be rolled down to protect the interior from summer-afternoon heat.

Tired and knowing she had a busy day ahead of her in the morning, Alyssa automatically checked locks and lights and then made her way into the bedroom. Tomorrow she would take her money down to the bank, and tomorrow evening she would call the hotel in Las Vegas and explain to Jordan why she would be a day late arriving.

Her own ready acceptance of the affair into which

she had plunged so heedlessly still left her feeling strangely out of tune with herself. But as she crawled into bed that night, Alyssa knew she had every intention of being on the Saturday-morning plane to Vegas. The lure of Jordan Kyle was more than she could withstand. Sleep that night brought visions of a golden-eyed man with wonderfully sensitive hands, and Alyssa gave herself up to the dream as she had given herself up to the man.

THE WORLD SHE CHOSE TO THINK OF AS "real" resumed with an unappealing rush the next day as Alyssa walked into her office and found Hugh Davis using her personal hotpot to heat water for his morning coffee. It wasn't that Alyssa was at all selfish with the hotpot. She wasn't. She just didn't particularly care for Hugh Davis. That he was the only other contender for the promotion she was seeking made her feel guilty for not liking him, however, and she silently gritted her teeth and smiled.

"Good morning, Hugh. Is the office pot broken again?" She nonchalantly stuffed the purse containing the thousand dollars into the lowest drawer of her desk, hoping she wasn't drawing undue attention to it, and slipped into her seat. The neat summer-weight suit in honey beige that she wore accented not only her slenderness but also her professional image. Her auburn hair was smoothed away from her face and held with two tortoise-shell clips behind her ears. She looked crisp and businesslike, the mysterious side of her that she took to Las Vegas well hidden.

Hugh Davis swung around slowly, pouring hot water into his cup as he turned to favor her with one of his sexiest smiles. At least, Alyssa thought, he obviously considered it sexy. For her part, she found it weak and superficial, just as she found the man. His pretty blonde wife, Cari, was welcome to him. Unfortunately for her sake, Alyssa wasn't too sure how much of him Cari actually got. Hugh Davis, according to the latest office gossip, was having an affair. No one knew with whom. With his tawny California handsomeness, Hugh no doubt found it relatively easy to attract women. He could be charming, had style and was definitely upwardly mobile. The combination was a natural winner in California.

"Morning, Alyssa. Nope, the office pot's not broken, but you know it never really boils the water properly, just gets it hot. I like it boiling for tea. I knew you wouldn't mind if I borrowed yours. How was your weekend?"

Alyssa hoped her involuntary flinch didn't show. She was going to have to get used to the automatic Monday morning question. Everyone inquired politely after everyone else's weekend.

"Just fine," she returned brightly. "How about yours?"

"Oh, fine, fine. Went sailing," Hugh replied absently, setting down the pot. Alyssa had begun to distrust the speculative look in his eyes that seemed to appear there more and more frequently when he happened to glance in her direction. She hoped he wasn't considering the prospect of making a pass at her.

"McGregor's going to want the final results of that statistical analysis we did for the new generation of transistors we tested last week. The client is expecting the results tomorrow," Alyssa reminded him in an effort to keep the conversation on a business footing.

"The data's ready to go into the computer. We should have it run by this afternoon." Hugh shrugged. "What time do you want to go over the results with me?"

Alyssa stifled a sigh and tapped her pencil impatiently on her desk. There was nothing she could do to avoid the consultation, of course. They had worked on the project together, and they would have to package the final report together. "How about three o'clock."

"Sure. Unless you'd rather do it this evening after work?" he offered with an ingratiating smile that thoroughly annoyed her.

"I prefer to get my work done during working hours," she returned sweetly.

"Ah, but budding managerial talent should make it clear to the boss that overtime is accepted, even welcomed. Managing isn't supposed to be a nine-to-five job, remember," he taunted lightly.

"I'll leave it to you to pursue that theory. I happen to believe that one of the signs of good management is getting the work done on time without having to put in extensive overtime!"

"Well, we'll just have to see which of us is taking the right tack for impressing McGregor, won't we?" Hugh drawled, sauntering toward the door. "Don't worry, Alyssa, when I get the promotion, I'll remember your attitude toward working outside regular hours," he promised kindly as he let himself out of her office.

Alyssa frowned thoughtfully at the closed door. As usual, she couldn't be sure if Hugh was only teasing or really up to something. The man might be shallow and superficial in some ways, but there was no doubt in her mind that he was quite devious. She wished she hadn't felt obliged to invite him for Friday night.

But if she had not invited Hugh and his wife, the rest of her office friends would wonder if she was deliberately excluding them because of the competition for the promotion. Ah, the complications of running her *real* life, she thought with a half-humorous sigh. Deliberately, she pulled the computer printout on her desk toward her. Here was the true joy of her job, she thought with satisfaction. She could lose herself in the beauty of the math that awaited her.

She didn't emerge from the intricacy of the mathematical model she was studying until noon, when, with secret satisfaction, she clutched her purse tightly all the way to the bank and deposited the thousand dollars.

She saved the phone call to Las Vegas until that evening, after she had eaten a light meal of quiche and salad accompanied by a glass of chilled Chablis. The thought of hearing Jordan's voice so soon brought a smile to her lips as she dialed the hotel number.

The smile was gone a moment later as the front desk informed her that Mr. Kyle was not in his room.

"May I take a message?" the polite voice on the other end inquired.

"No, that's all right, I'll call back later." He was probably at dinner, Alyssa decided, glancing at her watch. And after that he would hit the tables. Actually, he probably didn't spend much time in his room at all. If she didn't reach him when she tried later, she would have to leave a message and let him call her.

Another attempt at nine o'clock also proved fruitless. She would try once more before she went to bed, Alyssa decided. She'd rather not leave a message if she could catch him in the room instead.

But the call before bedtime proved fruitless, too. Jordan must be out working. Well, she'd try again tomorrow evening.

Two hours later, when her phone did ring, it brought

her out of a sound sleep, but her head was already clearing as she picked up the receiver. Perhaps Jordan had decided to phone her? Coming wide awake at the thought, she answered eagerly.

"Hello?"

There was only a dead silence on the other end of the line. Disgustedly, Alyssa hung up and unplugged the phone. The last thing she wanted to be bothered with tonight was pranksters or obscene phone callers! With the phone out of commission, the rest of the night passed in blissful silence.

The next evening, she dialed the hotel and automatically asked for Jordan's room by number.

"I'm sorry, our records show that Mr. Kyle has checked out of that room, madam." was the polite response.

"Checked out!" Surely he hadn't left Las Vegas? A chill of genuine fear went through her at the thought. The idea of seeing Jordan Kyle again next weekend had become the focal point of her days and nights. Thoughts of the exciting fantasy waiting for her on the weekend made everything around her brighter and more enjoyable. It even made it possible to tolerate Hugh Davis! Now the promise of the waiting illusion was being sliced to shreds, and the sickening reaction Alyssa experienced in the pit of her stomach told her how important that illusion had become.

Then a thought struck her just as the clerk was

trying to say good-by. "No, wait! Please, could you check your guest list for Mr. Kyle's name? I realize he's checked out of that particular room, but there's a possibility he might have asked for another."

"Very well, madam. One moment please."

Alyssa chewed her lips anxiously during the long moment that ensued, praying her hunch was correct. Jordan couldn't have left. He just could not have *left!* He had to be there, waiting for her return. The realization of how damp her palms were and how fast her heart was beating was frightening. Until that moment, she hadn't fully acknowledged to herself how important her affair with Jordan Kyle was. What had happened to her? Not only had she become embroiled last weekend in what she would normally have characterized as the most tawdry of weekend arrangements, she was sitting there a nervous wreck over the possibility that she would not be able to repeat the arrangement *next* weekend!

"Hello? Yes, we do show Mr. Kyle as having moved to another room. If you'll hold on, I'll connect you."

Alyssa swallowed, feeling dizzy from relief. "Thank you." The words came out in a particularly heartfelt manner.

Again, however, there was no answer, and this time Alyssa decided to try leaving a message. It would probably be easier for Jordan to get in touch with her, anyway. Their current working hours were making it too difficult to connect.

"Would you please leave a message for Mr. Kyle saying that Alyssa called and that she has remembered a previous engagement on Friday night. She'll arrive Saturday morning instead. He can call me at this number." Hurriedly, she rattled off her Ventura phone number and hung up.

That should do the trick, she decided. Jordan would get her message and call to find out what had happened. She would explain about Friday night and tell him how much she was looking forward to seeing him on Saturday. With a nod of satisfaction, Alyssa headed for bed with a biography of women mathematicians she had been reading.

When the phone rang an hour and a half later, she was still reading, immersed in the story of Hypatia, a mathematical scholar in ancient Greece. Instantly, the excitement began to flare in her veins as Alyssa reached for the receiver.

It died down to utter disgust as she once again was treated to a silent line. She was certain someone was listening on the other end, but not about to give whoever it was any encouragement, she unplugged the phone for the second night in a row. If this continued, she'd call the phone company.

Determinedly, she went back to the biography of the brilliant Hypatia, who had turned down numerous offers of marriage by claiming she was already wedded to the truth. Being "wedded to the truth," however, apparently had not stopped her from engaging in several love affairs.

Alyssa smiled to herself, reading between the lines as she looked back across the centuries. Hypatia had probably never married for the simple reason that she had never found a man who understood and appreciated her both mentally and physically and to whom she was equally attracted. Her scholarly work was renowned even during her own time, and Alyssa was enraged to discover that the poor woman had somehow become a political pawn between two rival factions and had been set upon and murdered by a street mob.

Just before she slipped off to sleep that night, Alyssa wondered what Hypatia would have done if she'd been fortunate enough to encounter a true soul mate during her adventurous lifetime. No doubt she would have plunged headlong into an affair and, perhaps, even marriage. No, perhaps she wouldn't have gone quite as far as marriage. The higher levels of mathematics were undoubtedly demanding enough to preclude the need for a mate. Even at the modest level at which she worked, Alyssa could see how the study of mathematics could consume and involve the truly brilliant.

As good as she was at her own work and as intrigued as she could become by math in general, Alyssa knew she lacked that kind of ability and dedication. If the right soul mate came along for her, she might be willing to consider marriage again. Assuming, of course, she reminded herself dryly, that the soul mate was equally interested in the institution.

Who was she kidding? Jordan Kyle had told her quite bluntly that men in his profession did not acquire wives and families. He ought to know by now. After all, he was nearly forty and had never married.

And there was no question that marriage to a professional gambler would ruin her present career. On that unhappy note, Alyssa fell asleep.

Jordan did not call back Wednesday evening. Alyssa waited until well after ten o'clock, and then she could stand the suspense no longer. Once more she dialed the Las Vegas hotel. She could only hope the desk clerk wouldn't recognize her voice or that she would be blessed with a different clerk. There was nothing more embarrassing than to have someone think you were chasing a man!

"Yes, Miss Chandler. Mr. Kyle did pick up your message. We gave it to him last night. Will there be anything else?" It was the same clerk, damn it!

"No, no, that will be all." Feeling very wretched, Alyssa hung up the phone and sank back into the cushions of her white couch. Jordan had picked up her message the night before. He hadn't been able to reach her then because her phone was unplugged but why hadn't he called this evening?

She was consumed with fresh fears and a host of

new doubts. She knew so little about the man. What if he were involved with someone else tonight? Why should she think that a man who had lived so long in that night world wouldn't play by its rules and customs? Why should Jordan spend his evenings alone, waiting for her return?

Las Vegas was a city of beautiful women. They flocked there to become showgirls, dancers, cocktail waitresses and hustlers. They came to attach themselves to the high rollers who could give them exotic presents and a sense of excitement. Jordan Kyle would be a prize in that world. And he must be aware of that fact. Winners were the ultimate heroes in Las Vegas.

By Thursday evening, Alyssa had convinced herself Jordan had found someone else. She alternated between rage and despair. *Why didn't he call?* Her pride would not let her dial the number of the hotel one more time.

On Friday morning, she told herself there was no way her pride would let her take that Saturday flight to Las Vegas, either. What a fool she had been!

The dinner party that evening was to be a buffet. Her boss and most of her coworkers had been invited. With her usual efficiency, Alyssa had done much of the preparation on Thursday evening, throwing herself into the project in an effort to erase her unhappiness over the ruined weekend. Friday afternoon, she left work a little early to take care of the finishing touches.

"It's not as if the great love affair of the century has come to an end," she scolded herself forcefully as she prepared the papaya, avocado and artichoke salad. "You only had one weekend with the man. For heaven's sake, you should be thanking your lucky stars that it didn't go beyond a single weekend!"

But there was no point thanking one's lucky stars when you didn't really believe in luck. Alyssa set the plates and silver on the serving table, arranging the Sonoma County Chardonnay and the Napa Valley Merlot wine bottles attractively behind the glassware.

Jordan believed in luck. Gritting her teeth, Alyssa remembered the way he had told her to drop the quarter in the slot machine that first night. He'd said something about believing in luck when one had been in his world as long as he had. He must have been feeling lucky to have picked up a woman so easily for the weekend. No doubt his luck had been just as good Sunday night after she'd left!

The chafing dish was ready for the pastas and smoked salmon dish, and the mushroom tart looked delicious. Alyssa surveyed the final preparations and was unable to summon up the satisfaction she ought to have been feeling. All she could think about was the anger that grew steadily inside her. Visions of Jordan with another woman, one who had made him decide to ignore his original plans for this weekend, flitted through her mind.

Damn it, she ought to be grateful! *Grateful!* Think how much worse she would have felt if she'd spent another weekend with him and then realized how faithless he was! This way at least she'd been warned in time to cancel her return flight. What would she have done if she'd arrived at the airport in Las Vegas this evening and found no one waiting for her? Alyssa winced and went into the kitchen to heat the crusty French bread.

Half an hour before her guests began arriving, Alyssa dressed, not really thinking about what she chose from her closet. The blouse was beautifully pleated down the front and along the full, full sleeves. It was of white silk with a neat black collar and wide black cuffs. Automatically, she slipped on black velvet trousers with a high waist that defined her slenderness and a pair of small, black patent-leather slippers. With her hair brushed into two shining auburn curves that framed her face, she turned once to glance in the mirror. Her thoughts were so full of the pain and outrage she felt that she missed entirely the effect she made in the mirror. For with the dashing black and white outfit, she had managed to create unconsciously a charming parody of a casino dealer's uniform, right down to the neat black bow tie.

The guests began arriving early. Alyssa was glad to see the first of her coworkers arrive because it gave her an excuse to throw herself into being the perfect hostess.

"I told Alice I wanted to get here early so we could see the sunset." Dirk Banning grinned as he escorted his attractive, middle-aged wife out onto the front porch.

"This house is made for summer-evening entertaining!" Alice exclaimed, charmed by the sight of beach and sky. Alyssa graciously put a drink in the woman's hand and made a polite remark.

The house *was* perfect for entertaining, she thought a few minutes later as the others arrived and immediately gravitated toward the porch with its spectacular ocean view. People loved the open vista, and the restless sea seemed to inspire conversation and a convivial atmosphere. With the assistance of the setting and a determined effort on her part, no one would guess the rage that seethed inside her.

Her boss, David McGregor, handsome still at sixty-three, arrived accompanied by the gracious, silver-haired woman who was his wife. Alyssa was in the process of greeting them both in the open doorway when she glanced up and saw the last couple arriving. The gleam of feminine hatred in Cari Davis's eyes as she came up the steps beside her husband, Hugh, caught Alyssa totally off guard.

She had only a few seconds in which to be sure of the expression in the other woman's face, and then it was gone, hidden behind a beautiful mask. No one else even noticed. Almost immediately, David McGregor was turning to greet his other employees, his jovial attitude giving no indication of whether he favored Alyssa or Hugh for the promotion that was in the offing. Years of experience in the world of corporate management had given McGregor a polish that completely belied the ruthless ability underneath. At this stage of the game, no one would be able to hazard a guess as to which of the two he would ultimately recommend for the open managerial slot.

Under cover of the flurry of polite greetings, Cari Davis turned to smile at her hostess. Only Alyssa seemed to realize that the smile never reached the other woman's eyes. "Covering all the angles, are you?"

"I beg your pardon?" Alyssa glanced at her blankly, not understanding the waves of cold dislike emanating from the other woman.

"Oh, I was just referring to the fact that you're making sure your future career is well protected regardless of whether it's Hugh or yourself who gets the promotion," Cari retorted lightly, turning back to smile brilliantly up at McGregor.

Alyssa remembered to close her mouth just as Mildred McGregor said something about the view. "You're just in time for the sunset," Alyssa told the other woman quickly. "Let me get you a drink before you go out onto the porch. What will you have?" My God, she thought as she poured the requested drink,

Cari Davis must be very anxious for her husband to gain that promotion. So anxious that she suddenly hated Alyssa? They had never been close friends, but there had always been conventional politeness between them on the various occasions when they came into contact with each other. Never had she been aware of such outright dislike on the part of the other woman.

Clearly, she was going to have to tread warily, Alyssa decided as she shepherded the last of her guests out onto the porch and passed around a plate of cream cheese and chutney canapés. She had no wish to become embroiled in an embarrassing skirmish with Hugh Davis's wife!

She was deeply involved in a discussion with Mildred McGregor on the care and feeding of ferns when the doorbell chimed one last time.

"Excuse me." She smiled politely, stepping back into the living room and heading for the door, a tiny frown drawing her auburn brows together. Everyone she had invited had already arrived. Surely a neighbor wasn't complaining about the noise already?

"I'm sorry if we're disturbing—" Alyssa began brightly as she flung open the door. But the remainder of the automatic apology died on her lips as she stared up at the apparition on her doorstep.

"Jordan!" she exclaimed, stunned.

"Good evening, Alyssa," he murmured in a

dangerously polite voice. "Don't stand there looking as if you've just seen a ghost, sweetheart. Didn't I warn you once not to make the mistake of thinking I was an illusion?"

He was, she realized belatedly, quite furious.

CHAPTER FIVE

"Didn't you…" Alyssa delicately moistened her dry lips with the tip of her tongue and tried again. "Didn't you get my message?"

She didn't seem to be able to move, her hand clutching the edge of the door for support. He stood in front of her, all dark, masculine intimidation in a black suede jacket, dark slacks and black shirt. The brown hair seemed almost black, too, in the fading light, and the golden eyes gleamed like those of a hunting car at night. Alyssa's first instinct was to run, just as she would have run from a real night prowler.

"Of course I got your message," Jordan growled gently, stepping over the threshold and forcing her back a couple of paces. "That's why I'm here instead of waiting for you at the Las Vegas airport."

"Jordan, I don't understand." Alyssa's head moved in unconscious denial of his very real presence. "You never phoned back. I expected you to call after you got my message." Eyes wide and anxious, she stared up at him, seeking some sort of explanation.

Jordan put out a hand, and his strong, aware fingers stroked the line of her throat once. "I didn't call," he explained with cool precision, "because what I really wanted to do was beat you senseless after I got that message. The telephone simply wasn't adequate for a full expression of the way I was feeling."

"Jordan!"

"I waited until I had overcome the urge to strangle you before I decided what to do next. I told myself that I should just forget about you, that a woman who casually remembered 'previous engagements' after making a date with a man wasn't worth beating, let along pursuing."

"But I wasn't trying to change my mind about the weekend!"

"When I cooled down a little and had a chance to think things over, I began to realize what was really going on in your head," he continued in a dark, quiet, utterly relentless tone. "And that's why I'm here tonight."

"I don't understand," she wailed, feeling threatened and intimidated and generally abused when by all rights she should have been the one demanding explanations. "If you think you're going to get away with beating me—"

"That part might or might not come later," he advised laconically, his eyes flickering over her speculatively. "Depending on how I feel after I've taken you to bed!"

"Jordan, this is ridiculous. I can't stand here listening to you make threats! I'm entertaining my boss and my coworkers this evening!" Alyssa gasped. Take her to bed? "You're supposed to be in Las Vegas," she wound up uncomprehendingly. And that was where he was supposed to make love to her. Las Vegas. Not here in her home in Ventura! Not here in her other life.

"Ah, yes, the 'previous engagement,' I presume?" he drawled, glancing out through the open windows at the crowd of people hovering cheerfully on her porch.

"It wasn't a lie," she defended herself hotly. "I'd had this buffet planned for two weeks. I simply forgot about it when I was getting ready to leave Las Vegas last weekend. I phoned you as soon as I could to explain, but you were very difficult to get hold of!"

"I was busy," he retorted simply.

"I'll bet!"

"Exactly what I was doing. Betting. It's my profession, remember? But you were busy remembering that you have another life and other commitments that come before an affair with a man you met one weekend in Las Vegas, weren't you?"

"Jordan, it was the truth! I didn't just dream up this buffet party on Monday morning as an excuse not to go back to Vegas tonight!"

"No, I believe you," he gritted, and then went on perceptively. "I'm sure this party was planned long in advance and it really did just slip your mind for a while. But you remembered as soon as you got back here because this is where the most important part of your life takes place, isn't it, Alyssa? This is your real world. You must come to Vegas to play once in a while, but you always hurry back home to your job and your friends and your 'previous commitments' when you've finished playing. Only this time you made a mistake, sweetheart. This time you left behind a man who doesn't want to be a weekend playmate for you. I'm not going to let you casually adjust your time with me so that it doesn't conflict with your 'previous engagements.'"

"Will you stop saying that!"

"Previous engagements? They're your words, remember? They were on the note you had the hotel clerk give me."

"Can't we talk about this later?" Alyssa pleaded helplessly, feeling at a total loss. She had been priding herself on how well she could juggle her two separate worlds, but now they had collided, and she didn't know what to do.

"Sure," he shot back with caustic indifference. "We can talk about it after dinner." He glanced toward the buffet. "What *is* for dinner, by the way? I'm starving."

"Jordan," she squeaked. "You can't stay here for dinner! I've got my boss and everyone I work with out there on that porch!"

"Not anymore." He smiled blandly, glancing past her shoulder toward open sliding-glass doors. "One of them has just come inside. Good evening," he went on politely to someone standing behind her. "I'm Jordan Kyle. I appear to be the late arrival."

"You're in luck," David McGregor proclaimed jovially as he came forward to shake the newcomer's hand. "We've barely begun to make inroads on Alyssa's terrific food. David McGregor. I'm Alyssa's boss at Yeoman Research."

For an instant of endless vertigo, Alyssa watched in horror as Jordan and her boss shook hands. It had happened. Her fantasy life and her real life had met. My God, she thought dazedly. What have I done? Visions of her career going down in flames left her momentarily paralyzed. If McGregor realized he was greeting a professional gambler and that Alyssa had spent a weekend with him in Las Vegas…that she had spent several weekends in Vegas…

Desperately, she pushed aside the image of mounting disaster. Nothing short of sheer inspiration would save her now. To her unending astonishment, it came.

"I'm so glad you could make it, after all, Jordan," she managed with a brilliant smile that would have done credit to a professional actress. "I know Mr. McGregor and the others will enjoy meeting you." She turned away from the wicked light in Jordan's golden eyes to say very brightly to her boss, "Jordan's a very busy man, and I was afraid he wouldn't be able to get here. An expert in probability theory, you know. One of the best in his field. I'm sure you'll enjoy talking to him. He's been recently engaged in a hush-hush research project over in Nevada."

"Oh, so you're in the same field as Alyssa, are you?" David McGregor nodded wisely at the younger man.

"Why, yes, as a matter of fact," Jordan returned smoothly, his gleaming gaze still on Alyssa's desperately composed features. "We have several parallel interests."

Oh, God. Was that a promise of vengeance she saw in that threatening gaze? "Wouldn't you like a drink, Jordan?" Anything to distract him, even temporarily. "Come on into the kitchen and I'll fix you something."

"That sounds delightful. It's been a rather long and extremely frustrating week," Jordan murmured.

"I know the kind," David said with a chuckle. "I'll see you out on the porch after Alyssa gets your drink for you, Jordan. Hurry. You don't want to miss the sunset. She's got a fabulous view from here."

"I'll be right there," Jordan promised, glancing with polite invitation toward his reluctant hostess. "Perhaps a Scotch and soda?" he prompted a little too gently.

Wordlessly, Alyssa swung around and made for the kitchen bar she had set up for the evening. When she reached for the bottle of Scotch, however, her fingers trembled, and Jordan reached across the low counter to take it firmly from her hand.

"An excellent brand," he approved, pouring a generous drink for himself. "And since I'm not working this evening, there's no reason I shouldn't enjoy myself along with the rest of your guests." He glanced up challengingly. "Is there? Being, as I am, one of the most respected men in my field." He lifted the glass in salute and downed a healthy swallow.

Alyssa licked her lips once, trying to think. "Jordan, you must see that this is going to be awfully awkward for both of us."

"Not at all. I'm beginning to look forward to the re-mainder of the evening. Now, if you'll excuse me, I think I will go out and join your other guests. Wouldn't want to miss that sunset."

"Jordan…!" she called after him anxiously, but it was too late. With a soft, gliding stride, he was already halfway across the living room, heading for the porch. Helplessly, Alyssa stared after him and then reluctantly followed. What else could she do? She didn't know Jordan Kyle well enough to even make a guess at what he would do out there on her porch. It was rather like turning a wolf loose among a bunch of conservative sheep.

By the time she reached the porch itself, Jordan was already back into conversation with David McGregor and his wife. In addition, David was cheerfully introducing him to others. Alyssa cringed inwardly as she heard the words "probability theory expert," and then her attention was being captured by Cari Davis.

"Not putting all your eggs in one basket, I see," Cari murmured with a smile that would have frozen hydrogen. "Very wise. But, then, being a *professional* woman, I'm sure you've had plenty of experience at this sort of thing."

"I beg your pardon?" Blankly, her mind still on Jordan, Alyssa stared at her guest.

"I'm talking about your charming Mr. Kyle, of course. Always wise to keep a couple of men on the line at the same time, I imagine." Before Alyssa could ask her what she was talking about, Cari had moved off to join another group of guests.

Reality was turning into a crazy nightmare.

Unable to think of anything else to do, Alyssa grabbed a platter of canapés and headed grimly for the nearest cluster of people. For the next several minutes, she made herself act the part of the perfect hostess, trying desperately to keep her anxious gaze from veering toward the knot of people around Jordan Kyle.

"Oh, Alyssa." Mildred McGregor smiled, coming up behind her and reaching politely for a canapé. "There you are. I've been looking for you. I've just met your charming Jordan. Fascinating man. Who would have thought a professional mathematician could be so interesting? I must say, when I was in school, I avoided the subject like the plague. Strictly the liberal arts type. But your Jordan is very intriguing. And so amusing!"

"Amusing?" Alyssa repeated weakly. Almost simultaneously, there came a burst of delighted laughter from the group near Jordan, and she swung around nervously to stare at the far end of the porch.

"Yes, indeed. He's recently finished an overseas assignment, apparently, and he has some wonderful stories to relate. Excuse me, I must be getting back. Love these tidbits," she added, holding aloft the canapé she had just taken from Alyssa's tray.

What in the world did Jordan think he was doing? Alyssa stood, tray in hand, and stared at his dark head, bent attentively toward Lucy Chavez from the personnel department. Several other people stood around, too, and they all laughed again as Jordan responded to something the attractive young brunette said. Good grief! He was rapidly becoming the life of the party!

For the next hour, Alyssa felt as if she were walking a tightrope. The strain of waiting for imminent disaster was almost worse than the catastrophe itself would be when it finally arrived, she told herself. The suspense continued as she circulated among her guests, replenishing drinks and joining in the light conversation that characterized such events. Always she was conscious of Jordan's presence, waiting for the truth to come out and appall everyone. In her growing anxiety, she found herself reaching for a third glass of wine before she remembered to announce dinner.

"Please help yourselves," she instructed with false cheerfulness as the happy group began to troop toward the buffet table. Jordan was among those choosing plates and a napkinful of silverware, she realized grimly. He was playing his new role to the hilt!

The last to go through the buffet line, Alyssa found it extremely difficult to work up any enthusiasm for the pasta and salmon dish or the mushroom tart. She took a little salad on her plate and was reluctantly adding a chunk of crusty French bread when Jordan's smooth, dark drawl made her whirl around.

"Let me get you a glass of wine to go with that, Alyssa," he murmured, holding his full plate in one hand and deftly pouring out some chilled Sonoma County Chardonnay with the other. Such skilled, knowing hands. The memories returned in full force. "Something wrong, sweetheart?" Jordan inquired blandly, handing her the glass. "You're blushing."

"No, no, nothing. Jordan, please," she hissed, "what do you think you're doing?"

"Having a good time." He paused as if considering his own words. "Make that a *very* good time. I can't remember ever having attended a party quite like this one."

"Like this one? That doesn't make any sense! This

is a perfectly normal, perfectly routine sort of buffet dinner party!"

"For you. Not for me." He smiled to himself, glancing around the room. "All these people have respectable, well-paying careers with fringe benefits and retirement plans and medical insurance. And they think I'm one of them, thanks to you. In fact, thanks to you, they think I'm a leader in my field."

"What in the world are you talking about? Jordan, I don't understand you. How much longer are you going to go on like this?" She pleaded with her eyes, desperate for some clue as to when he would say the words that would ruin the evening and her career.

"I'm enjoying myself, honey. Don't you like to have your guests enjoy themselves? Now why don't you come on over to the couch and we'll have our dinner together." He sniffed appreciatively. "Smells delicious. Your talents seem to be quite endless."

There was nothing else to do but follow him over to the white couch and join several other guests who had settled in the vicinity.

"Fantastic pasta dish, Alyssa," Ned Grummond commended as he forked up an oversized portion. "Don't let me forget to get the recipe from you before I leave tonight." Ned's portly figure gave ample evidence of his long-standing interest in food. But he apparently had other interests in life, too, Alyssa realized as he turned a beaming smile of welcome on

Jordan. "So you're an expert in probability theory, eh?"

"I make my living using various aspects of the theory, yes," Jordan returned easily, settling down onto the couch and reaching up to assist Alyssa. The moment the strong fingers closed around her arm, she knew there wasn't any option except to sink down beside him.

"Have to confess I've never been much good at math myself." Ned sighed and was joined by several ruefully agreeing voices from those around him. "All I can do to balance my checkbook, I'm afraid. But it's always kind of fascinated me, you know? I've always admired people who have a head for numbers. I know Alyssa here uses her background in the statistics area. How about you? What exactly does an expert in probability theory do?"

There was a murmur of interest from some of the others, and several people glanced inquiringly at Jordan. Do something, Alyssa, she screamed silently at herself. This is your future that's on the line. If Jordan answers this question accurately, it's going to shock this whole roomful of people, including your boss.

"I believe I mentioned earlier that Jordan isn't really free to discuss his work," she began bravely. "You know how it is with government projects."

"That's okay, honey," Jordan interrupted smoothly.

"I think I can talk about my subject without giving away any state secrets. Ned has asked a very good question, and you know how I love my field."

She cast a desperately appealing glance at him and realized there was nothing she could say or do to halt the inevitable. "Are you sure you wouldn't care for another helping of mushroom tart?" she tried valiantly, mostly for the sake of trying.

"I've got plenty, thanks. Actually, Ned, I'm afraid probability theory has its roots in the disreputable world of gambling," he went on conversationally.

Ned chuckled, and so did several of the others. "I hadn't thought about it, but I suppose there must be some direct applications."

"Precisely," Jordan nodded approvingly. "In fact, legend has it that it was the curiosity of gamblers that first gave rise to the questions, which, in turn, gave rise to the beginnings of the theory."

"What kinds of questions?" Lucy Chavez inquired, leaning forward interestedly and managing to display a fair amount of bosom in the process.

"Oh, questions such as the ones some gamblers asked Galileo over three centuries ago. They wanted to know why a throw of dice turns up certain sums more often than others. Professional gamblers were still asking similar questions a hundred years later, and a lot of mathematics which developed to describe the theory of chance have a lot of useful applications, but it's still often easier to understand them if you think in terms of a familiar game of chance."

"Like roulette?" Lucy interjected.

"Good example," Jordan murmured appreciatively. "Or craps or blackjack or any one of the several other games. You'd be amazed at how many people who gamble have no understanding at all of the theory behind the games."

Alyssa choked on a small sliver of her French bread. Instantly, Jordan was all concern, slapping her heartily on the back until she managed to gasp that she was all right. The interruption, however, didn't slow him down at all, and his listeners were fascinated.

"For example," he went on cheerfully, reaching into his pocket and extracting a coin. "If I toss this quarter ten times and it comes down heads each time, a lot of people will think that because of some 'law of averages' the eleventh toss is far more likely to turn up tails than heads."

"Isn't it?" Ned Grummond demanded curiously, his eyes following the coin as Jordan idly flicked it into the air and caught it on the back of his hand. "I mean, after having turned up heads so many times in a row, it's *bound* to eventually turn up tails."

"In my profession, that's sometimes affectionately known as the Monte Carlo fallacy." Jordan grinned, displaying the coin, which had indeed landed heads. "The truth is, every toss of the coin is independent of every other toss. Assuming the quarter is a correctly made, evenly weighted coin, it's just as likely to turn up heads on the eleventh toss as it was on the first or sixth or eighth toss. A fifty-fifty chance." He flipped the coin again, catching it with a sureness that made Alyssa wince. "If you were betting on the outcome, you'd want to remember that every toss has a fifty-fifty chance regardless of how many tosses have been made or how many times heads has already come up."

"Dessert anyone?" Alyssa asked quickly, surging to her feet hopefully.

"Sounds great, honey." Jordan smiled before turning back to his audience. "Oh, and while you're getting it, do you think you could rustle up a deck of cards?"

"Cards?" She looked at him, horror-struck.

"Cards," he repeated firmly. "You must have a deck around. Everyone keeps one. A lot of things are easier to demonstrate with a card deck."

When she realized everyone was looking toward her expectantly, Alyssa lost her nerve. "I'll see what I can find." She fled toward the kitchen, an angry red coloring her cheeks. She couldn't believe this was happening. A sense of unreality began to take over, providing a welcome numbness.

By the time she had dished up cheesecake and produced the deck of cards, Alyssa was, in fact, becoming quite fatalistic. The evening had to end in disaster. There was no alternative. Given the inevitability of the outcome, why let herself grow tense each time Jordan responded to another question. After all, a catastrophe was a catastrophe. When it came, it would be quite final.

She looked on with her new fatalistic calm as Jordan shuffled the cards for his latest demonstration of the theory of probability. Almost idly, she wondered if anyone in the crowd watching him would notice the expertise of the shuffle. Those damned good hands were going to be her downfall, she thought. Those strong, beautifully shaped fingers were going to pull down the fragile bricks and mortar of her career just as surely as if they had planted a bomb.

"Where did you run into Kyle, Alyssa?"

She started a little as Hugh Davis appeared at her shoulder. "He's a, uh, colleague of mine, Hugh. We've known each other on a professional basis for some time." It sounded weak even to her own ears.

"Really? I'd say he considers himself a bit more than a professional colleague, wouldn't you? He's been calling you 'honey' since he came through the door."

"Jordan's very casual about things like that," she managed a little grimly. Why should Hugh Davis care one way or the other how Jordan addressed her? At that moment the man in question glanced up from across the room where he was dealing a "demonstration" hand of cards for a group of interested people. The golden eyes snagged hers, and something decidedly menacing flickered in his gaze. In spite of her numbed sense of reality, Alyssa shivered. With the still-functioning feminine intuition that was born into every woman, she read the expression in his eyes very accurately.

Jordan Kyle didn't like her proximity to Hugh Davis.

As if he had any right to object after what he's done to me tonight, she thought vengefully.

Hugh Davis moved perceptibly closer, bending his head in what must appear a too-attentive fashion. "Correct me if I'm wrong, but something tells me you're going to be in for a lecture after everyone else goes home tonight. Your friend Kyle may be casual, but that look he's giving me is definitely not one of easygoing camaraderie!"

Alyssa gave herself a small, inner shake and moved away from him. "If you'll excuse me, Hugh, I think Mr. McGregor needs another slice of cheesecake." It was only as she deliberately turned to head for the buffet table that Alyssa realized Jordan wasn't the only one in the crowd eying her proximity to Hugh Davis. Hugh's wife, Cari, was watching the small tableau with a sullen expression that made Alyssa uneasy.

Would this horrible evening never end?

But it did eventually, and much to Alyssa's stunned

surprise, it did so without the disastrous finale she had been expecting from the moment Jordan Kyle had entered her home.

To her everlasting astonishment, the wretched buffet party drew to a quiet, happily reluctant close as guests finally began to take their leave shortly after midnight. And each and every one of them bid good night to Jordan as if they were delighted to have encountered him.

"I hope we'll see you around, Jordan," David McGregor announced enthusiastically, shaking Jordan's hand in farewell. He flicked a paternally amused glance at Alyssa, who was quietly ushering people out the door. "I assume that's a foregone conclusion, though, isn't it?"

"I think so," Jordan returned suavely, following McGregor's glance. "I have no intention of letting Alyssa out of my sight for any lengthy stretch of time. You know how women are, sir. A man needs to keep his eye on his property or he runs the risk of its getting lost, strayed or stolen."

Alyssa shot him a distinctly unamused glance before turing to say good-by to Lucy Chavez and her date. "Good night, Lucy. I'll see you Monday morning. Thanks for coming."

"Oh, you know I always enjoy your parties, Alyssa," the other woman said, laughing. "But I must say that I never dreamed the evening would be so

An Important Message from the Editors

Dear Reader,

Because you've chosen to read one of our fine novels, we'd like to say "thank you"! And, as a special way to thank you, we're offering you a choice of two more of the books you love so well, and a surprise gift to send you – absolutely FREE!

Please enjoy them with our compliments...

Pam Powers

el off Seal and
Place Inside...

FREE GIFT
EDITOR'S SEAL
THANK YOU

What's Your Reading Pleasure...
ROMANCE? _OR_ SUSPENSE?

Do you prefer spine-tingling page turners OR heart-stirring stories about love and relationships? Tell us which books you enjoy – and you'll get 2 FREE "ROMANCE" BOOKS or 2 FREE "SUSPENSE" BOOKS with no obligation to purchase anything.

Choose **"ROMANCE"** and get **2 FREE BOOKS** that will fuel your imagination with intensely moving stories about life, love and relationships.

Choose **"SUSPENSE"** and you'll get **2 FREE BOOKS** that will thrill you with a spine-tingling blend of suspense and mystery.

Whichever category you select, your 2 free books have a combined cover price of $11.98 or more in the U.S. and $13.98 or more in Canada.

And remember. . . just for accepting the Editor's Free Gift Offer, we'll send you 2 books and a gift, ABSOLUTELY FREE!

YOURS FREE! We'll send you a fabulous surprise gift absolutely FREE, just for trying "Romance" or "Suspense"!

Order online at
www.FreeBooksandGift.com

THE EDITOR'S "THANK YOU" FREE GIFTS INCLUDE:

- ▶ 2 Romance OR 2 Suspense books
- ▶ An exciting surprise gift

YES! I have placed my Editor's "thank you" Free Gifts seal in the space provided at right. Please send me the 2 FREE books which I have selected, and my FREE Mystery Gift. I understand that I am under no obligation to purchase anything further, as explained on the back of this card.

PLACE
FREE GIFTS
SEAL
HERE

Check one:

	ROMANCE
	193 MDL EE39 393 MDL EE4M

	SUSPENSE
	192 MDL EE4L 392 MDL EE4X

FIRST NAME	LAST NAME

ADDRESS

APT.#	CITY

STATE/PROV.	ZIP/POSTAL CODE

▶ DETACH AND MAIL CARD TODAY! ▶

(ED1-HQN-06) © 1998 MIRA BOOKS

The Reader Service — Here's How It Works:

Accepting your 2 free books and gift places you under no obligation to buy anything. You may keep the books and gift and return the shipping statement marked "cancel." If you do not cancel, about a month later we'll send you 3 additional books and bill you just $5.24 each in the U.S., or $5.74 each in Canada, plus 25¢ shipping & handling per book and applicable taxes if any.* That's the complete price and — compared to cover prices starting from $5.99 each in the U.S. and $6.99 each in Canada — it's quite a bargain! You may cancel at any time, but if you choose to continue, every month we'll send you 3 more books, which you may either purchase at the discount price or return to us and cancel your subscription.

*Terms and prices subject to change without notice. Sales tax applicable in N.Y. Canadian residents will be charged applicable provincial taxes and GST.

educational!" She smiled at Jordan. "Perhaps if my math instructors had made their lessons as entertaining as you make yours, I would have gotten more out of the classes back in high school!"

"Thank you, Lucy," Jordan said with a sincerity that caught Alyssa's attention. He meant it, she thought to herself. He really enjoyed the compliment.

It was one of many he received as the remainder of the guests made their way out the door. By the time the last one had departed, Alyssa was forced to concede that Jordan Kyle had been the evening's most popular attraction.

And every single one of those departing guests seemed convinced they had spent the evening being entertained by a preeminent expert in the field of probability theory. Dazed, she acknowledged the fact that not one of them had apparently guessed Jordan's true occupation. Alyssa shut the door behind the last guest with a mixture of wonder and apprehension flooding through her.

There was only Jordan left now in the quiet room. Slowly, she turned to confront him, her eyes narrowing as anger began to break through the artificial, fatalistic calm that had overcome her during the latter half of her evening.

"I suppose," she began seethingly, "that you think you're rather clever!"

He eyed her for a long moment, and she wondered

what he was thinking. His expression gave no clue. "I *know* I'm rather clever," he corrected too mildly as he strolled over to the white couch and threw himself down on it in a lithe sprawl. His eyes gleamed. "I make my living by being rather clever, remember?"

"Jordan…" She felt the danger in him very clearly now.

"So this is how you spend your time when you're not amusing yourself in Vegas, hmmm?" He glanced meaningfully around the living room with its litter of glasses and plates. "This is your real world?"

"Part of it," she made herself say very bravely.

He nodded. "I enjoyed dropping in on your world tonight, Alyssa. I liked passing myself off as a mathematical scholar. I liked having people admire my abilities just as if my skills were quite respectable. It was a complete change of environment for me." He surveyed her taut expression. "And I think I like the idea of returning to your world whenever I feel like it."

"Jordan! You can't mean that," she whispered, aware of the mounting tension in the room. "What are you trying to say?"

"That I'm going to be right behind you when you shuttle back and forth between your two worlds, Alyssa. You're not going to relegate me to Las Vegas or Reno. I'm not a tame consort who will agree to stay out of sight and out of mind until you happen to work me into your schedule. I'm not going to play the other man on weekends while you maintain a normal, proper sort of life here in Ventura during the week. If you want to come and play in my world, you'll have to let me come and play in yours!"

"Jordan, listen to me. I realize you're probably still a little upset about the way I postponed my arrival in Vegas until tomorrow," Alyssa began, some instinct warning her that angry as she was, it might be wiser to placate him tonight.

"Upset? Not at all," he drawled, watching her the way a leopard watches its prey. "Haven't I just explained that I had a great time this evening?"

She sucked in her breath, summoning up her courage. "I think we ought to talk this all out in the morning."

He was up off the couch in one easy movement, gliding toward her with cool menace. "What an excellent idea. We'll save the discussion for the morning. That leaves us the remainder of the evening to clarify another matter."

"Jordan, wait!" Eyes widening with sudden anxiety, Alyssa instinctively backed away from him.

"I have been waiting," he said simply. "All week, I still haven't decided yet whether or not I'm going to beat you, but I sure as hell intend to take you to bed, my reckless lady gambler. I want to make certain you understand that I'm going to play a very real role in your life."

Panic overwhelmed her, but it was too late to run. Jordan moved, catching Alyssa up in his arms before she could even think of escape. Then he started down the corridor to her bedroom without any hesitation whatsoever.

CHAPTER SIX

IT TOOK ALMOST TWENTY SECONDS FOR Alyssa's shock to wear off, and by then it was too late. Jordan was already striding through her bedroom door with his captive securely in his arms when her outrage finally overcame the stunned paralysis.

"Put me down," she demanded, her sea-colored eyes more green than gray as they reflected the full force of her rising fury. "I mean it, Jordan. Let me go this instant! You have absolutely no right to treat me this way. I won't tolerate it! Do you hear me?"

"I hear you. Do you always sound this shrewish when things aren't going exactly as you planned them?" He seemed more interested than alarmed, and Alyssa felt anger sizzling in her blood stream.

Anger and something else. Would there always be an underlying element of passion coursing through her whenever this man touched her? That thought made her even more furious, and she used her gilded coral nails with sharp effect on his shoulders. Since she had slid her fingertips inside the collar of the suede jacket, he had no protection against the savage little attack. "Damn you, Jordan, I won't be treated like this!"

He sucked in his breath and she sank her nails into the fabric of his dark shirt, and then he simply opened his arms and let her fall. The unexpected release startled her, and she parted her lips to cry out. But the bed came up to meet her before the small sound escaped, and she sprawled awkwardly on the thick, sand-colored quilt.

"You," he announced grimly, leaning forward to plant a hand on either side of her, "are going to learn a few facts about me tonight that apparently escaped you last weekend. The most important of which is that as long as I'm in your life, *I'm really in your life,* every aspect of it. You can't relegate me to the weekends and come back here to Ventura to flirt with that Davis character."

"I wasn't flirting with him!" Struggling to sit up and finding it impossible, Alyssa lay trapped within the cage of his arms, her eyes glinting with resentment and, perhaps, a small tinge of fear. She didn't want to acknowledge the fear, however. She refused to acknowledge it. Her determination not to do so led her to add rashly, "But even if I were, you'd have no right to object!"

His face hardened, and his eyes resembled more than ever those of a hunting cat. Where was the charmingly polite gambler? The man who had woven a spell of seduction last weekend? The man who had so entranced her guests tonight? Alyssa lay very still and tried to retain her nerve.

"He was watching you every time you moved, and I'm not the only one who noticed. His wife was aware of what was going on, too. Are you having an affair with Hugh Davis? An amusing little interlude to occupy you during the week until the weekend rolls around and you can hop a plane to Vegas?"

"For the last time, I'm not having an affair with the man!" But she was beginning to understand some of Cari Davis's hostility. Did Hugh's wife really believe her husband was having an affair with Alyssa? There wasn't time to worry about that angle, however. Alyssa had her hands full dealing with her primary accuser. "But for the record, who the hell are you to stand there demanding explanations? How did you spend your week, Jordan?"

"I was working!"

"And after work? Did you pick up a lady to help you while away your off-duty hours? Or are you going to tell me you didn't keep yourself occupied this last week?" she snapped, remembering all those nights when he hadn't returned her phone calls. Her imagination had worked overtime during those long evenings. "Las Vegas is a city of beautiful women, and they all love winners!"

"Jealous?" he asked with savage curiosity.

"Why should I be? We have no claims on each other!" she tried to say with lofty dismissal, but inwardly she cringed because he was making no effort to deny her accusation.

"You're wrong on that score. I sure as hell am staking a claim on you, and I intend to see to it that you honor that claim. Whatever is going on between you and Davis is over as of tonight. Understood? The only affair you're involved in from now on is the one you're having with me. And it's not just a weekend arrangement!"

He moved abruptly, straightening and beginning to peel off the soft suede jacket. His eyes never left Alyssa's wary, tense face as he absently draped the jacket over the back of a nearby chair and began unbuttoning the dark suit.

Temporarily free, Alyssa sat up on the quilt, curling her legs under her protectively. She could feel the blood racing through her veins and was unable to shake the heady combination of passion and anger that was swirling through her. "Jordan, I won't let you do this to me. If you think you can casually show up on my doorstep and…and force yourself on me, you're out of your mind!"

"Not surprising," he agreed laconically, tossing the shirt in the general direction of the jacket and beginning to unclasp the leather belt at his waist. "I think

I've been half out of my mind for a good portion of the week. I even lost money on Thursday night. Money I didn't intend to lose."

Alyssa blinked, aware of the significance of his admission. "I'm…I'm sorry about your concentration," she began, tentatively, edging carefully away to the opposite side of the bed.

"Don't worry, I intend to restore my peace of mind!" He yanked off the expensive calfskin shoes he was wearing and then stepped out of the dark slacks. Along with the slacks went his one remaining garment, a pair of snug cotton briefs.

Alyssa swallowed as his hard, lean body emerged from the clothing. She knew a primitive urge to run and an equally primitive need to touch the blunt, sleek planes of him. He was aroused, and the soft light of her bedside lamp threw dark, dangerous shadows across his smoothly muscled thighs and the contours of his chest.

"Jordan, please, wait." Her right hand lifted in a pleading gesture. "We need to talk. You know that. There are too many misunderstandings. You're angry, and so am I. This isn't any way to solve our problems."

He fit his strong hands to his waist, and a flash of cool amusement lit his gaze. "I suppose we could try dialing a marriage counselor. Except that we're not married."

"This isn't a joke!"

"Well, given the fact that we can't call in outside arbitration, we'll just have to solve our problems in the old-fashioned way." He leaned forward slightly, one hand going to the buttons of her black bow tie.

Alyssa reacted, realizing that there was nothing she could say now that would stop him. With a violent little twist, she leaped from the far edge of the bed and was on her feet across from him in an instant. Her bow tie dangled from his fingers as he straightened to pin her with his gaze.

"Are you going to try running?" he asked almost conversationally.

"Don't threaten me, Jordan." Her breath was coming more quickly now as she realized the peril of the situation. She couldn't take her eyes off him. Or perhaps she didn't care to do so, she told herself silently. He was between her and the door, and the odds of getting safely back out of the room was definitely not in her favor. Jordan was far too good a gambler not to realize that fact, too.

"I'm not going to threaten you," he said almost gently, surprising her by sinking down onto the quilt with his back to her. He gazed musingly down at the strip of black silk in his fingers as if it fascinated him in some way. "I'm going to make love to you. There's a difference, you know."

Alyssa moistened her dry lips. "Not as long as you're going about it in this highhanded fashion!"

He glanced back over his shoulder, a wry curve to his mouth. "Come here, Alyssa." His eyes were gleaming, and his voice was exquisitely deep and gentle.

She blinked, taken aback by the change in his approach. Quite suddenly, he was the infinitely seductive man she had known in Las Vegas, and the knowledge that he could turn the dangerous charm on at will made her deeply wary. "I don't think so, Jordan. Not until we've talked."

"Then talk to me," he invited huskily, threading the black silk through his fingers. Alyssa found herself following the small action, hypnotized. Those hands... "Talk to me and tell me you understand how much I want you."

"Do you, Jordan?" she heard herself breathe. "Do you really want me?"

"So badly that I swallowed my pride to track you down here in Ventura," he said simply.

"I thought it might have been your pride which brought you here," she countered, wondering desperately what was happening to her will to resist. Her eyes still followed the way his sensitive fingers toyed sensually with her bow tie.

"If I'd listened to my pride," he said carefully, "I'd still be in Vegas. I had to come and find you tonight, Alyssa. I couldn't bear the thought of your being out with some other man."

The desire and longing was clearly visible in the depths of his eyes, and they drew Alyssa like a magnet. She might have been able to go on resisting him if he had stuck to the macho approach, but this sensual, captivating honesty tugged at all her senses. If she had gone to Las Vegas tonight on schedule, they would by now have been lying in each other's arms. How could it be any different having him here? This man could weave magic around her, and realizing that didn't seem to make it any easier to fight it.

"There isn't any other man, Jordan," she stated quietly.

"Davis?" he prompted softly.

"He and I are after the same promotion at work. We know each other strictly on a business basis. That's all there is to it," she whispered.

He continued to gaze at her over his shoulder for a moment longer, and then his head inclined faintly in acceptance of her explanation. "There wasn't any other woman during the week, honey."

Her fingers curled into the palm of her hand as she stood very still. "I...I wondered. When you didn't call."

"It was my pride that kept me from calling. Not another woman."

"Oh, Jordan," she sighed.

The hand with the strip of silk laced between the fingers was held out to her. "Now will you come here, Alyssa?"

"Are you…" she broke off and tried again. "Are you still angry with me for not going to Vegas tonight?"

"Do I look angry?" he countered softly, his hand still extended across the bed. "Come here, Alyssa, and let me show you how I really feel tonight."

The last of her wariness dissolved in the face of his gentle seduction. Slowly, Alyssa knelt down on the bed and put out her hand to touch his. He touched her palm lightly, drawing her toward him with such a gossamer pressure that she was almost unaware of what was happening until she found herself kneeling less than two inches away from him. Then the lure of his broad shoulder overcame her, and she trailed her fingertips down the curve of his arm.

"I'm not angry, Alyssa. Not any longer. I need you too much." He turned her palm upward, moving his lips across it in a warm caress. "I've been needing you all week."

"Did you really lose last night?" she whispered, loving the touch of his mouth on her vulnerable palm. The thought of being capable of wrecking his concentration sufficiently to cause him to gamble badly was intoxicating. It gave her a heady sense of power and an equally pervasive feeling of tenderness.

"I lost. But I won't lose tonight, will I, sweetheart?" He moved his lips to the inside of her wrist holding her hand with the lightest of touches. The silk bow tie dropped unheeded to the quilt as Jordan shifted his weight in a subtle manner.

The next thing she knew, Alyssa felt herself being lowered slowly until she was lying on her back and he was ranged alongside her. The warmth of his naked body was like a fire on a cold night, infinitely inviting and full of promise. She could feel the blatant thrust of his manhood against her leg, and she shivered.

"Oh, Jordan, I thought about you all week," she confessed softly, her arms going up around his neck in a gesture of acceptance. Or was it one of surrender? Alyssa didn't want to think about the nuances of the action just then.

"And you've been on my mind ever since I had to put you on that damn plane back to California," he muttered. Slowly, he undid the buttons of her pleated tuxedo blouse, working with care and anticipation. He wasn't going to hurry this, she realized. As if he had read her mind, his mouth crooked slightly as he pushed aside one edge of the blouse and bent to kiss the swell of her breast above the neat white bra. "I'm in a mood to make it last the rest of the night. I want to compensate myself for all the long, lonely evenings this past week."

Alyssa trembled a little beneath the feather-light kiss, and her fingers flexed, catlike, in the darkness of his hair. "You're sure you're not still angry?" she questioned one last time. There had been a real threat in him when he'd arrived on her doorstep this evening and then again when he'd watched her with Hugh. It was hard to believe all that male vengeance had truly disappeared.

"I want you too much to be angry tonight." He lifted his head, his fingers slipping along the high waistband of her black trousers. "But this time I'm going to make very, very sure of you, sweetheart," he added huskily.

She shifted with a trace of unease. "I don't understand."

"You will by morning." His mouth closed over hers in a slow, drugging kiss that seared away the last of her uncertainty.

Alyssa sighed into his throat and gave herself up to the embrace. This was what she had been dreaming of all week. This man of math and magic was the lover she had never quite dared to believe existed. How could she resist him tonight?

His teasing, gently arousing fingers traced erotic patterns across the skin of her stomach before unfastening the black trousers and slipping them down to her feet. Alyssa stirred restlessly as the fires within her began to build. She stroked him again and again, unable to get enough of him. Her hands moved over his shoulders and along his lean hips to the hard, muscled planes of his buttocks. There her nails sank lovingly, enticingly into him, and his groan of response was as satisfying as the finest wine.

"Tonight was not a fantasy night, was it?" Jordan murmured on a hoarse thread of humor as he touched the fabric of her plain white underwear. "No black lace and satin?"

"And no bordello-red bedroom, either," she countered. "Miss them?"

"I shall remember that night with the greatest pleasure, but no, I don't miss the trappings of the fantasy. The only thing I'm concerned with is the part that's real. You."

He kissed her again as his palm slid up along her inner thigh and closed over the heart of her desire. Alyssa gasped as the warmth of his hand penetrated through the thin white cotton that still shielded her. With her mouth still trapped beneath his, she arched her hips instinctively.

"Wildfire," he whispered throatily. "You're like wildfire under my hands."

She couldn't answer. She was too conscious of those incredible hands, and her body was too caught up in the web they were spinning around her. When he drew small circles with a bold finger against the white cotton, she moaned far back in her throat and clung to him.

Reaching up, he captured one of her wrists and lowered her hand to the heat of his thighs. "I've been dreaming of your touch all week. Make my dreams come true."

The full strength of his masculinity slipped into her palm, and she heard him suck in his breath. With trembling fingers, she explored the heavy, probing hardness of him, and a tremor went through his body. Uttering a groan of mounting need, he buried his lips against her throat while his finger slid under the edge of her cotton panties.

"Jordan!" The word was a plea as he deliberately teased the sensitized softness between her legs.

He muttered something dark and sensual, and then he lowered his head to take the taut peak of one breast in his mouth. The tender tug of his caress there sent wave after wave of longing through her system. When she was a writhing flame beneath him, he began to work his way down her body, his tongue moving over her damply.

"Only for me," he rasped. "I want you like this only for me. My God, woman, you're driving me out of my head!" He nipped a little savagely at the delicate silk of her inner thigh, and the small punishment sang excitingly through her senses.

"Now, Jordan. Please. I need you so."

But he held off a little longer, kissing her so intimately, she cried out with wonder.

"Tell me," he muttered thickly as he tracked searing kisses back up to her breasts and her throat. "Tell me you're mine. Tell me you belong to me, sweetheart."

She trembled at the unmistakable element of

command in his words. Tonight he intended to be sure
of her, he'd said. Was this what he meant? Was he
going to force an acknowledgment of her own surrender from her? But she couldn't seem to think of any
way around the truth in that moment.

"Jordan…?"

"Tell me!"

"Oh, yes, Jordan. Yes!" She clutched at his shoulders, urging him to cover her fully and let her absorb
his hardness into her softness. It was all that mattered
just then. "I want you so!"

Jordan looked down at the woman lying so passionately in his arms, begging for him, and he knew he
could wait no longer. All week he had been remembering the way she came alive beneath him, the satisfaction and the glory he took in first driving her wild
and then taming her completely. A part of him had
wanted to tease her and torment her for hours tonight
before allowing either one of them the satisfaction
they craved. But he had been a week without her, and
the uncertainty during that time had made him too
hungry. His need of her was too great to postpone the
inevitable any longer.

"Tell me once more," he whispered urgently as he
held himself less than an inch away. "Tell me you
know you're mine. That you belong to me!" God!
After what he had been through this past week, waiting
and wondering and berating himself for having fallen

for such an elusive creature, he needed to hear the words a thousand times before morning. When she moaned beneath him and closed her eyes in anticipation, he told himself he would take the words again and again from her that night. He would be absolutely certain that by the time dawn came, she knew she was his. He would not be a weekend fantasy for her!

"Yes, Jordan," Alyssa whispered passionately, her hands flowing over him as she begged him to come to her. "I'm yours. Please be mine."

"Alyssa!" Jordan surged against her body. How could he refuse that last request? All he wanted to do in that moment was make them one.

At the moment of complete possession, Alyssa felt the breath stop in her throat. Her body reacted to the sweet invasion on a thousand different levels, acknowledging its need and longing for this man who, by all rights, should have been a stranger.

But he wasn't a stranger. Here in her arms, he was the other half of herself, Alyssa realized vaguely. The thought came and went, driven out by the lightning that was flashing through her. Jordan was stamping the imprint of his body on hers in no uncertain terms. As he drove her powerfully toward the final brink, a part of her wondered at the intensity of his lovemaking. When he mastered her softness with his overwhelming passion he knew he would force her to give herself up to it completely. He would brook no halfhearted surrender.

Clinging helplessly to the strength of him, Alyssa found herself skyrocketing toward the ultimate conclusion, and the extent of Jordan's power over her senses was almost frightening, even in that tumultuous, primitive moment. Recognition of that power made her cry out unconsciously in a husky protest.

"No! Jordan, no…"

He must have heard and understood the strange note of fear and defiance in the broken words because his mouth moved to hers, silencing the small sound forcefully. Not savagely, she reflected later when she remembered the incident, but with absolute determination. He would allow her no escape from the complete possession he was claiming.

With whatever protest she might have made sealed forever, Alyssa gave herself up to the pounding conclusion of his lovemaking. She knew he felt the first delicate tremors within her almost as soon as she herself was aware of them, for he locked her close and whispered heated words of encouragement as he pushed her over the edge.

Jordan clearly savored the evidence of her satisfaction for as long as possible before he let himself be swept over the same precipice. Alyssa, still lost in the world of sensation, heard his exultant shout and knew the roughness of his teeth against her bare shoulder. Instinctively, she clung to him.

Long moments later, she slowly surfaced to hear the

sound of her name being repeated in a rhythmic, crooning fashion, as if it were a litany.

"Alyssa, Alyssa, Alyssa."

She opened her eyes slowly to find Jordan watching her, his head nestled beside hers on the pillow. His body was still connected to her own, and there was a sheen of perspiration on his forehead. She was damp, too, Alyssa thought vaguely. Damp and beautifully lethargic, wonderfully satiated. The golden eyes burned into her own.

"I frightened you," Jordan stated.

"Perhaps. A little." She didn't have the energy just then to argue the point.

"Why?" The question was almost stark.

"I feel…" She hesitated, honestly searching for the right words. "Out of control when you're around." Her head moved restlessly on the pillow, auburn tresses fanning out on the white fabric. "I don't understand how it is you can seduce me so easily. I just don't understand."

His fingers closed over hers, entangling. "It works both ways, you know."

"It's different for a man."

"No," he countered. "I won't buy that. I'll admit that sex can be more varied, perhaps, carry a lot of different meanings with different women. But when it happens the way it does between you and me, it's just as shattering for the male as it is for the female."

"Shattering?" She looked at him uncomprehendingly. "You feel *shattered?* What a strange way to put it. You're so perfectly seductive. It must be cool and calculated and deliberate. This is the second time you've set out to seduce me, and both times I felt as if you were spinning a web around me. I felt lured and drawn and…and helpless. Tonight, just before"—she paused awkwardly, glancing away from the intensity in him—"just before the end, I suddenly realized what was happening and how powerless I was. How out of control. It frightened me."

"It's like gambling when you can't calculate the odds or count the cards," he murmured. "You're so in control of your working world and even of your fantasy world that it scares you when you encounter something you can't completely manage, doesn't it?"

He was right, she realized, and in the vulnerable aftermath of their lovemaking, she couldn't find the strength to deny it. "When…when we met in Las Vegas, you seduced me just as easily, but when I left, I felt I still had everything under control. You were part of the fantasy world, but I could leave that world behind when I returned to California. I still felt relatively safe."

His fingers tightened on hers. "You mean as long as I stayed in my proper place, you still thought you could juggle a fantasy life and a real life."

"It seemed possible," she agreed with a sigh, wondering what was going to happen now.

"Then I showed up on your doorstep tonight, and you realized your carefully separated worlds were about to collide," he concluded a little roughly.

"Yes."

"I warned you before you left Vegas not to think of me as an illusion," he reminded her grimly.

"Yes," she said again. But she hadn't heeded the warning.

"I saw the fear in your eyes several times during the course of the evening, you know," he went on in a falsely conversational tone. "I knew I'd really thrown you for a loop by showing up here in Ventura. But I was furious with you for having relegated me to another side of your life. I had expected to arrive just in time to keep you from going out on a date with another man. I hadn't expected to find you giving a party. I wasn't sure what I was going to do at that point, and then you solved the problem very neatly by introducing me as some damn expert in probability theory."

Alyssa winced, remembering her burst of "inspiration." "You certainly carried off the role very well!" she muttered caustically.

"I had fun," he told her simply. "I thoroughly enjoyed myself tonight, Alyssa. Just as you enjoyed yourself last weekend in Las Vegas playing the role of mysterious lady gambler."

"But you...I..." She stumbled over the protest,

seeking a way to explain the difference. "When we spent the night together in Las Vegas—"

"You still felt an element of safety because you knew you'd be leaving that world behind. Tonight, when I made love to you, it was happening in your safe, controlled, *real* world, and you knew you weren't going to be able to leave it neatly behind this time," he concluded for her on a fierce note. "Well, from that standpoint, perhaps you were right to be a little scared. Because you can't package me up and ship me back to Vegas, honey. I'm the only lover in your life now, Alyssa. And I'm going to make sure that's true for both of your lives!"

She turned her head quickly on the pillow, her lips parted to say words that had not yet formed in her head. The words never emerged. He sealed her mouth with his own, crushing her softly back against the pillow....

The omnipresent sound of the ocean filtered slowly into Alyssa's consciousness along with the light of a new morning. She blinked sleepily, aware of the heavy weight beside her in the bed and the unaccustomed sensation of warmth from another body. Slowly, she allowed herself to focus on Jordan's intriguingly ruffled hair as he lay asleep, facing her. The memories of the night washed over her, and she stared at the hard lines of his face, which were only partially softened in sleep.

Last night, he had spent the long hours of darkness making certain she would not ever be able to push him out of her life again. She had known that was his goal, sensed his desire to burn himself into her so thoroughly she would never be able to resist him regardless of which of her worlds he entered.

It was the deliberate way he had done it that left her feeling so high-strung and uneasy this morning. He had carried her into the bedroom with every intention of achieving his goal. Looking back at it, Alyssa was certain that when he had switched gears and resorted to a more tenderly seductive, gently luring approach, it had been deliberate. He had played her emotions the way he played cards.

What was this man doing to her? What was going to become of her if she did not extricate herself from his spell? Who he was and what he was threatened everything she had worked so hard to establish during the past few years. Her career at Yeoman Research would come to a dead standstill if it were ever discovered that she consorted with professional gamblers and even engaged in the reckless pastime herself. Professional gamblers were dangerous, untrustworthy and disreputable. They were not to be entrusted with positions of responsibility.

And were they to be trusted on more personal levels? Alyssa shivered faintly as she slipped silently off the bed and reached for her yellow robe. How was she going to get herself free of this man? How could she get the situation back under control? She didn't dare risk another scene such as the one at the party last night. If Jordan insisted on invading her real world as he had last night, it was only a matter of time before her luck ran out.

Her luck. She had never really believed in luck until she'd met Jordan. Now she was definitely beginning to wonder about the phenomenon. If one accepted the premise that it existed, one had to also accept the premise that there was both good luck and bad. Meeting Jordan Kyle could only be a piece of incredibly bad luck for her.

It wasn't until she found herself wrenching the faucets in the shower with a particularly violent twist that Alyssa realized just how much resentment was brewing in her that morning.

No, that was putting it mildly. She was furious. That man in her bedroom had no right to invade her life and turn everything upside down. He had no right to have such power over her senses. No right to be able to make her respond in his arms so thoroughly. The feeling of powerlessness, of being out of control of her carefully structured world, sent a chill of fear through her once again. She had to get free of Jordan's magic web!

By the time she finished the shower, she was feeling tense, ready to snap or slash like a small, cornered animal. When she opened the door into the bedroom, the yellow robe wrapped securely around her, Jordan stirred lazily amid the sheets and propped himself up on his elbow to give her a slow, satisfied, remembering smile.

"Good morning, sweetheart. You're up bright and early. Part of your normal routine?"

The slight reference to her "normal" world was made deliberately, she knew. Everything Jordan Kyle did was undoubtedly deliberate. Calculated. Such qualities were essential to the career he had chosen, weren't they?

"It's late," she returned, not meeting his eyes as she strode firmly across the off-white carpet to her closet and began pulling out a pair of jeans and a long-sleeved shirt in jewel blue. "You'd better get dressed."

He groaned, sinking back down onto the pillow. "Do I detect a shade of asperity in your tone?"

"At least you didn't wake up to find me going through your wallet."

"Ouch. That was unkind. I was desperate that morning."

With her clothes bundled in her arms, she hurried back to the bathroom, feeling more than a little desperate herself.

Jordan waited until she reemerged, completely dressed, before he flung back the covers and got slowly to his feet. She saw the speculative, assessing gleam in his eyes as she swept past him toward the bedroom door, and then she was safely in the hall.

She would have to fix breakfast for him. There was really no way around that. And then, she promised herself as she violently sliced a grapefruit in half, they would have to talk. The situation between them had to be settled. It could not be allowed to go on any longer. The danger was far too great. What a fool she had been to contemplate an affair with the man!

The doorbell chimed just as she finished sectioning the grapefruit, and with a renewed pang of anxiety she went to answer it. Who could it be at this hour? Would she have to explain Jordan's presence? What she did was her own business, of course, but still, it would be easier if she didn't have to admit that Jordan was not only a distinguished colleague but also a lover.

With such thoughts whirling in her head, she opened the door to find Ray Burgess standing outside. Surprise was in her voice as she greeted him.

"Ray! What are you doing here? I wasn't expecting you. How are Julia and the baby?"

The pleasant, lanky young man on her doorstep grinned, blue eyes sparkling as he held up a check. "They're just fine, of course. And I'm here only because I'm here on business."

With a flourish, he proffered the check. "A thousand dollars, Alyssa. I sold three paintings this past week, and when it came to paying bills, you were on the top of my list."

She stared at him, shocked. "A thousand dollars, Ray? But I can't take this! I mean, you don't have to worry about the money, please. I…"

"Alyssa, I want you to have it. I couldn't have made it without you a couple months ago. I insist you take it, and no arguments." He stepped forward and spontaneously kissed her cheek while stuffing the check into her reluctant hand. "Don't worry, it's not going to bounce," he added, chuckling. "And there will be another one next month."

It was Jordan, his dark voice at its most dangerous, who responded to the remark. "That check may not bounce, but you sure as hell will, all the way to San Diego, if you don't take it back and make a very quick exit. And if you try to bring another check by next month, I'll take you apart."

CHAPTER SEVEN

AS THE LOW-VOICED THREAT REVERBERATED among the three people standing in Alyssa's doorway, she and Ray Burgess both swung to face the man who had issued it. There was a moment of appalled silence while Alyssa groped for an explanation, but it was Ray who plunged in, anxious to pacify.

"Hey, it's okay," he murmured with an attempt at an engaging smile. He held up his hands in a gesture of innocence. "She's not my lady, if that's what's worrying you, mister. I'm a happily married man. With a kid, no less!"

"Those qualifications haven't stopped a lot of men from writing out checks for other women in the past," Jordan growled softly. He slanted a disdainful glance at the younger man. "But this other woman is now private property. She won't be taking your money now or in the future."

"Jordan, stop it!" Alyssa finally gasped as she found her tongue. "You have no notion of what's going on here. This is between Ray and me. It does not involve you!"

He flicked her a disgusted look, as if she weren't very bright. "Everything you do now involves me. Remember?"

"We can run through that argument at a more convenient time," she said angrily, her fingers curling into fists as she glared up at him. "For the moment, I would appreciate it if you would kindly step out of a situation that does not concern you!"

"Alyssa, let me explain it to him," Ray began. He turned back to face Jordan. "I'm Ray Burgess, and I…"

"I don't give a damn who you are," Jordan swore before Ray could get any further. "I want you out of Alyssa's home and out of her life. And take the check with you!"

"Stop giving orders in my house, Jordan!" Alyssa stepped between the two men, infuriated. On top of everything else, this scene was the last straw. "Ray is a friend of mine, and I will not allow you to stand there and yell at him!"

"I'm not yelling at him," Jordan pointed out very, very softly. "But I will definitely do some damage to him if he does not remove himself immediately. Is that very clear to both of you?" His attention was fully on Ray.

"Look, Jordan, or whatever your name is, if you'll just calm down, I swear I can explain everything."

"I'm not in a mood to hear explanations. That check you're trying to give Alyssa explains everything. Now get out."

Disgustedly, Alyssa turned away from the implacable Jordan. "You'd better go, Ray. I'll call you later, and we'll settle everything."

"You won't be calling him later," Jordan interrupted smoothly.

She flashed him a seething glance. "Please, Ray. It's all right. Just go."

"But, Alyssa, I can't leave you here to face him. He's irrational." Ray stared at her worriedly.

"I'm aware of that," she muttered. "But don't worry about me. I'll be all right."

"Are you sure?" He flicked an uneasy glance at Jordan.

"She'll be fine. Take her advice and leave," Jordan snapped.

"If you lay a hand on her, I swear I'll..." Ray began heatedly.

"I've already had my hands on every inch of her. And from now on no other man is going to have that privilege. Understood?"

"Jordan!" Alyssa felt the red rush into her cheeks. At that moment, she could cheerfully have throttled him if there had been any conceivable way of doing it. "How dare you say things like that?" she breathed, enraged. *"How dare you?"*

"That does it," Ray announced firmly. "I'm not leaving until we get this settled."

"Ray, please. Just go," Alyssa begged, sending him

an appealing look. "I'll take care of myself. Don't worry about me."

Her friend shifted uneasily. "Are you sure, Alyssa? You can come with me if you think you're in any danger here. We can wait until he cools down, and then…"

"You may stop discussing me as if I weren't present," Jordan drawled. "I assure you I'm very definitely here. Something Alyssa is having a little trouble understanding apparently. Get out of here, Burgess. And remember that Alyssa is now off limits to you or anyone else."

Nails digging into her palms as she tried to control her temper, Alyssa nodded at Ray. "Go on, Ray."

"You're sure?" He frowned.

"I'm sure."

"Well, at least let me leave the check…"

"No!" Jordan's voice cracked like a whip.

"No, Ray, please take the check. I don't need it. You don't have to give it to me, really!" Anxious now to get her friend out of harm's way, Alyssa began pushing him toward the step.

Reluctantly, Ray allowed himself to be pushed. Slowly, he walked out to his car, casting several suspicious glances back at the two in the doorway. Alyssa didn't close the door until he drove off. Then she slammed it and whirled to face Jordan. Scathingly, she raked his lean, solid form. He had put on the dark slacks and shirt he'd worn the night before, and it was easy to see why Ray had been reluctant to leave her alone with the man. He looked more than a little menacing, and his golden eyes glittered with cold promise.

"You're determined to barge into my life and tear it to shreds, aren't you?" she flung at him.

"Alyssa," he began grimly, only to have her slash across his words with the sharp edge of her tongue.

"You've just made a fool out of yourself and out of me! I hope to hell you're satisfied! Never have I been so humiliated! And you wouldn't even listen to a reasonable explanation, would you? Oh no! You had to blunder in like some sort of wild beast, wreaking havoc. You had no idea what was going on, and yet you took it upon yourself to interfere. Not only that, but you succeeded in thoroughly embarrassing me in the process!"

"Alyssa," he tried again, a strong warning tone underlining the word. "It was damn obvious what was going on. Who the hell was he to think he could buy you for a thousand bucks a month? How many others have you got on the string? What's the matter with you? Do you need money so badly that you not only hold down a full-time job but you gamble in Vegas and set up a stable of men to keep you in proper style?"

This time she silenced him with a sudden, vicious slap that left the imprint of her fingers against his cheek. The sound of the blow seemed to fill the living room. It was followed by a moment of terrible silence.

Then Jordan moved. One strong, skilled hand went out with the swiftness of a striking snake, capturing her wrist. He yanked her toward him until she was crushed against his chest.

"Who the hell is Ray Burgess? What's he doing in your life?" The words came out clipped and icy.

From somewhere, Alyssa found the courage to reply. In that single moment, she was more frightened of Jordan Kyle than she had ever been of anyone or anything in her whole life, but a remnant of common sense told her the only route to safety lay in explaining the situation as quickly as possible. Why on earth had she succumbed to the temptation to slap him?

"He and his wife are the reason I discovered Las Vegas."

Whatever the answer he had been expecting, that wasn't it. "What is that supposed to mean?"

"If you'll let go of me, I'll explain everything," she managed bravely.

He glanced down at the hold he had on the small, fragile bones of her wrist. Slowly, he unpeeled his fingers one by one until she was free. There was a red brand on her skin where he had been holding her.

Carefully, Alyssa disengaged herself, her hand going to the sore wrist. His eyes followed the small action, and she had the impression that he was a little shocked at the violence of the grip. "Ray's wife is a close friend of mine. We had an apartment together for a couple of years in Los Angeles. She's three years younger than I am. She met Ray almost a year ago when she came to Ventura to visit me. They're both struggling artists, and they fell in love almost as soon as they were introduced. Julia married him seven months ago when she discovered she was pregnant."

"Go on," Jordan ordered.

Alyssa's mouth crooked wryly. "Well, as I said, they're both a couple of struggling artists. No extra cash and no medical insurance. Do you know what it costs to have a baby in a good hospital with a first-class doctor these days? It can easily run to three thousand dollars or more. And Ray wouldn't have any less than the best possible care for his wife!"

"Oh, my God," Jordan muttered, eyes narrowing. "They came to you for a loan?"

"They didn't know where else to turn. Ray refused to go to his relatives because they've been so disapproving of his lifestyle. Julia simply doesn't have any relatives who could afford to help." Alyssa edged toward the kitchen as she spoke, and Jordan followed like a hunting panther.

"So they came to you for help?"

"Unfortunately, I didn't have that much ready cash on hand. My money was mostly tied up in the stock market, and the market's been such a disaster area lately that I hated to sell shares at such a loss if it wasn't absolutely necessary. The three of us spent an evening playing cards one night, discussing various possibilities, and I was winning game after game, as usual. It was only a friendly little game, no money involved. But I got to thinking later that I knew a lot about cards and dice and probabilities. I had studied them as object lessons for years. In addition, I seemed to have an intuition about numbers. I'm not sure it really has all that much to do with mathematics, this intuition. After all, there are a lot of mathematicians who can't gamble successfully." Her ex-husband had been one, she remembered.

For the first time since he had confronted Ray in her doorway, Jordan's expression softened slightly. "I know. And you don't have to explain about that feeling of knowing what the cards will do next. I make my living on that kind of intuition, remember?"

"You don't have to remind me," she snapped, annoyed. "I'm well aware of the fact." She reached for the two plates of grapefruit and set them down on the kitchen table. Through the window, the surf could be seen crashing on the sand. It was a charming scene on most mornings. But not this morning. Nothing was charming about this morning.

"Go on with the story," Jordan instructed, crisply, sitting down at the round, glass-topped table.

"There's not much left to tell. Once I had started

thinking in that direction, I couldn't wait to see if I could make it work. I didn't tell a soul where I was going or what I was planning to do. I just caught a flight to Vegas and plunged in with a stake of about two hundred dollars. By the end of the weekend, I had the three thousand. No one could have been more astonished than I was. I think, deep down, I hadn't really expected the theories and the intuition to work. When I got home that Monday, I phoned Ray and told him I'd had a small windfall in the market and that I would be happy to let him have the profits for Julia's medical care. The baby was born last week." Alyssa looked down at her own grapefruit as she took the remaining seat. "It was a little girl. They named her after me."

Even in the midst of her battle with Jordan, that thought made her smile. She had been delighted and unaccountably touched when Ray and Julia had given her the news.

There was a long silence from the other side of the table, and then the magic fingers swept out to cover her hand. "That must be nice," Jordan said very gently. "Having a kid named after you. No one's ever named a kid after me."

She glanced up to find him studying her with a new understanding in his eyes. For a few seconds, a strange communion flowed between them. Jordan, Alyssa realized abruptly, wasn't the only one who had denied himself a family because of his lifestyle. Hadn't she done the same for different reasons? She had been so intent on proving that she could be successful in her world of applied mathematics that nothing else had seemed to matter.

A good salary, a good job title, a house on the beach. Those comprised the elements of success at her end of the mathematical spectrum. For her father and her ex-husband, it had been prestige and recognition at the highest academic levels. But success in any world required certain sacrifices. Suddenly, she wondered if the ones she had made were worth the success they had brought her.

Jordan, too, must have made decisions along the line that had precluded his having a family. Professional gamblers didn't need that kind of excess baggage. Did he sometimes regret those decisions?

"Well, that's the story," she made herself say rather tartly as she dug into her grapefruit. The warm fingers, which had been idly caressing her hand, were withdrawn. It left her feeling a little bereft. Which was absolutely ridiculous, she told herself firmly.

"Not quite," he amended. "You got the money you needed for the emergency in which you were involved. But that wasn't the end of it, was it, Alyssa? After all, you went back to Vegas."

"Unfortunately!"

"That depends. Why did you go back, Alyssa?"

"You know why!" She didn't like being pressed

this way. He wanted her to admit something that she didn't wish to go into that morning.

"I know why. I just want to hear you say it," he goaded.

"I went back because I had fun, damn you! I went back because it was like having another world to escape to whenever I felt the need!"

"A fantasy world."

"Is there anything wrong with that?" she challenged.

He appeared to take his time considering the question. She felt like using her grapefruit knife on his throat. "Nothing *wrong*, precisely," he finally allowed judiciously. "But a bit reckless. Dangerous, perhaps."

"You don't have to tell me that," she grumbled. "I've already found out just how dangerous it can be!"

He shrugged that off. "But you had fun in my world, didn't you, Alyssa?"

"Yes," she bit out.

"Just as I had fun in yours last night."

She blinked uncertainly. That knowledge bothered her for some strange reason. Jordan had enjoyed himself last night. She had seen the pleasure in his eyes from time to time as he answered a question from one of the other guests or told a story that elicited their laughter. He had been playing the role of respectable mathematician, and it had obviously appealed to him.

It didn't bother her particularly that he had enjoyed

himself. What annoyed, worried and intrigued her was that a part of her had been happy for him. A part of her had taken pleasure in his pleasure, had wanted him to be happy. In spite of her anger and wariness, she realized she had found a curious satisfaction in having given him a measure of enjoyment by providing him with a new role to play. What a fool she was! This man had her tied in knots of silk!

"So am I going to get an apology at least?" she demanded brashly, anxious to put a stop to her current line of thought.

The lines bracketing the sides of his hard mouth tightened. "For kicking your friend Ray out the door when all he was attempting to do was pay off his loan? I'd say you got your own back when I let you get away with slapping me the way you did!"

"You're too generous," she snapped.

"I know," he agreed placidly. "I'm a gentleman, you see. A *scholar* and a gentleman. Thanks to you." He paused, peering at her as though debating something with himself. "Okay," he finally said magnanimously, "I'm sorry I didn't let you and Burgess explain everything at the door. Let's do everyone concerned a favor, though, and not make a practice of having strange men arriving bright and early on your doorstep with thousand-dollar checks in their hands. If you need money," he added a little gruffly, "I'll give it to you."

That infuriated her. "I don't need money! Yours or

anyone else's! I'm perfectly capable of paying my own way in life. I've got an excellent job and…and a way of making a little extra for the luxuries I want."

"It occurred to me you might be thinking of giving up gambling now that it's gotten you into such an uncomfortable situation," he returned blandly. "Is there anything else to go with this grapefruit?"

"This isn't a hotel, and I'm not room service!"

"Good lord. You really are in a hell of a mood this morning, aren't you?" he noted interestedly as he got to his feet and began searching through her cabinets. "Ah, here we go," he added as he discovered a box of cereal.

She watched him morosely as he puttered around her kitchen, finding a bowl and spoon and milk. "What am I going to do about Ray and Julia?" Alyssa finally blurted out, not knowing anyone else with whom she could discuss the problem. "I can't let them pay me back. That money I gave them was free. All it cost me was the price of a plane trip to Vegas."

He shrugged, returning to the table and pouring himself a generous portion of cereal. "That's one of the problems with making money the way we make it in Vegas. It can be a little awkward to explain. Especially since you're so anxious to keep the source secret. Maybe you could convince them it's a gift to your new little namesake?"

"I don't know. Ray and Julia are very proud. It was

hard for them to ask for help in the first place. If I refuse to let them pay back the money…"

"Then tell them the truth," Jordan suggested, plunging into the cereal with a large spoon.

"I haven't told *anyone* the truth about those Vegas trips! I'm afraid that once the word gets out, the wrong people might eventually find out and draw the wrong conclusions."

"Wrong people like your boss McGregor?"

"Yes!" she snapped in annoyance.

"Double lives can get very complicated," Jordan opined, golden eyes glinting. "Interesting, but complicated."

"This isn't a joke, damn it…!" But the remainder of her admonition was cut off by the ringing of the telephone. With an impatient movement, she got to her feet and stalked across the kitchen to where a yellow phone hung on the wall.

"Alyssa? Is that you?" came David McGregor's voice in response to her rather crisp greeting. "Glad I caught you before you went out for the day."

"Oh, yes, sir! Good morning, Mr. McGregor. I wasn't expecting to hear from you." Alyssa got out a little lamely, cursing herself for the too-abrupt way she had answered the phone. Automatically, she slid a glance across the room and found Jordan watching her.

"Well, Mildred and I were just sitting here saying what a pleasant evening we had last night, and we

were wondering if your friend Kyle was still in town?"
McGregor's friendly, ingratiating tones didn't fool
Alyssa for a moment. She had worked for this man
long enough to know that he rarely did anything
without a good reason. This Saturday-morning phone
call was totally out of the ordinary for him. Instantly
alert to the hidden nuances of the question, Alyssa
turned back to frown sternly at the wall in front of her,
thinking.

"Why, yes, as a matter of fact, he is still in Ventura,"
she admitted cautiously. "Please tell Mildred that I'm
glad she enjoyed herself," she added quickly in what
was undoubtedly a futile effort to get her boss off the
subject of Jordan Kyle. He ignored the red herring
completely.

"Excellent!" McGregor murmured genially. "Then
if the two of you aren't doing anything in particular
this afternoon, Mildred and I would like to invite you
over for a rubber of bridge. Around two o'clock, say?
Afterward, we can barbecue some steaks. How does
that sound? You and Jordan do play bridge, don't
you?" he inquired belatedly.

"Uh, yes," she said blankly, desperately trying to
figure out what was going on. This was a command
performance, and she knew it. McGregor did not routinely invite members of his office staff for bridge and
a barbecue on the weekends. And he wanted Jordan
there. Suddenly, everything clicked in her head. Jordan

was to be vetted. That was the only explanation that made any sense. "Yes, we do play, Mr. McGregor. That sounds delightful. Please tell Mildred I'll bring a salad."

His mission accomplished, David McGregor hung up the phone with a polite, satisfied-sounding farewell. Alyssa slowly replaced the receiver and remained staring at the wall, her hand still resting on the yellow instrument beside her.

"Something wrong?" Jordan inquired politely, still munching cereal.

"Do you play bridge?" she asked stonily.

"Not if I can avoid it."

"Well, you can't avoid it. Not today. And it's all your own fault." She swung around to confront him, her hands on her hips as she glared across the room. "That was my boss, and we have been invited to spend the afternoon with him and his wife, playing bridge and having a barbecue. Do you understand what that means?"

Jordan polished off the last of the cereal and sat back in his chair, reaching for the coffeepot on the counter behind him. "It means we've been invited for bridge and a barbecue. I didn't hear you trying to get out of it."

"Because I can't get out of it!" she stormed, striding back to the table and flinging herself down onto her chair. "McGregor wants us there, and as long as I'm trying to get that promotion, I am well advised to do as McGregor wants. You're the main reason for this sudden invitation, Jordan."

"I am?" He poured coffee for her and replaced the pot without glancing behind him. Such good hands. Perfect coordination in those supple fingers. Alyssa wondered if anything could disturb the sureness in those hands.

"Yes, damn it, you are. You're to be vetted this afternoon, Jordan. McGregor is curious about you. He wants to check you out." Alyssa's own fingers drummed in nervous impatience on the glass-topped table as she eyed her unwelcome guest.

"You mean he suspects I'm not who I said I was?" Jordan didn't appear overly concerned by that possibility, merely curious.

"I doubt that's the problem," she retorted. "You did an excellent job of passing for a respectable scholar last night!"

"Thanks. I thought I handled it rather well myself." He smiled at her over the rim of his cup.

Alyssa leaned forward, her brows coming close together in a ferocious frown. "I suspect he wants to know exactly what your plans are in relation to me," she told him very precisely, enunciating each word carefully.

"Ah!" Jordan's smile was in his eyes now, and Alyssa could have shaken him if she'd had the power to do so. "He wants to know if I'm going to lure you away from Ventura?"

"Probably. If he thought I was on the verge of getting married and leaving town, for example, it would certainly affect his decision of whom to promote, wouldn't it?" Alyssa shot back with saccharine sweetness.

"Most likely," Jordan agreed judiciously, sipping his coffee. His eyes never left her face.

"So we must make it very clear to him that you are not a threat," she concluded firmly.

"A threat?"

"You know what I mean. He must understand that I'm committed to Ventura for the foreseeable future. Which is only the truth. Jordan, if you don't behave yourself this afternoon and help me out of this mess, I swear I will nail your gambler's hide to my garage door!"

"Yes, ma'am," he murmured meekly enough. But his eyes were gleaming, and Alyssa didn't trust the look in them at all.

"I mean it, Jordan. I'll never forgive you if you ruin my chances of getting that job!"

"I understand," he said placatingly.

She sat back in her chair, eying him suspiciously. The man was actually looking forward to the afternoon, she realized dismally. He probably saw it as another chance to play at being the respected mathematician. "About the bridge game," she went on ruthlessly.

"Yes?"

"We will be partners, of course, playing against the McGregors. And we will lose, Jordan. Is that very clear?"

"If that's the way you want it."

"We will not lose badly. We will make it a close game; give them a run for their money…"

"We'll be playing for money?" Jordan asked brightly.

"That was a figure of speech. There will not be any money involved. The point is that I want to play a good, respectable game, but in the end I want the McGregors to win."

"Whatever you say," he agreed laconically. "Want some more coffee? No? Then come on, shrew, let's go for a walk on the beach. Maybe the sea breeze will blow you into a better mood."

He was on his feet before she could protest, reaching down to catch her wrist and haul her up beside him. Maybe he was right, Alyssa thought morosely as he led her firmly out the door and down onto the sand, where they removed their shoes. Maybe a nice long walk on the beach would clear her head and enable her to think. She was certainly going to need all her wits about her this afternoon as she handled the McGregors. Her career might very well depend on how adroitly she fielded her boss's subtle questions today.

"Feels good to be on a beach again," Jordan said, inhaling appreciatively. It was early yet, and they had most of the long, luxurious sweep of sand and sea to themselves.

"Your home is on the coast, isn't it?" Alyssa muttered, remembering the Oregon address on his driver's license.

"Ummm. It is, but I don't spend a lot of time there. It's just an address for me. A place to go when I'm not working." He led her along the packed sand near the water's edge at a brisk pace, his fingers wrapped securely around her wrist.

In spite of her own problems, Alyssa felt her curiosity rise. "It's not a home for you? A real home?"

"Just a place to go between casinos." He shrugged, glancing down at her. "Not like this place is for you. How long have you lived in Ventura, Alyssa?"

"Nearly four years now."

"Four years," he repeated thoughtfully. "When were you divorced?"

"When I was twenty-four," she responded shortly.

"Haven't you ever wanted to remarry?" he probed.

"Not particularly. I've been busy."

"Ah, yes. Building this famous career of yours."

"Is there anything wrong with that?" she charged tightly, her eyes on the sea's horizon. "After all, you've devoted your life to your career, too! You said you'd never been married."

"True. I never thought marriage would work very well in my case. It would take a very special kind of woman to accept a professional gambler as a husband, don't you think? It would take a woman who really *understood*. A woman who didn't mind the odd hours, the constant traveling, the endless motel rooms or the fact that her husband's job would not be particularly admired or respected by the vast majority of her friends and family. Most people consider gambling something to be done as an occasional fling. Something to do for an exciting, slightly naughty weekend once a year. People who do it more often are thought to be a trifle seedy, to say the least. Or sick with a compulsion," he added thoughtfully.

"In most cases that's a fairly accurate assessment," Alyssa pointed out. "Compulsive gamblers are sick. But you're hardly a compulsive gambler. You don't fit the stereotype, and you know it. You've chosen to make your living by your wits and your natural talent." She didn't know why she was defending him. After all, everything he had said about gambling was perfectly true. It was that very image of gambling that she feared so much, because all the stereotypes would be applied to her if it were to be discovered that she gambled as frequently as she did.

"Well, whatever the reality of my particular

situation, you have to admit I don't have the kind of job that would make me good husband material," Jordan observed dryly. "I guess you could say I've never married because of my career. Just as you haven't remarried because of your career."

She slanted a quick, uncertain glance up at him, wondering what was coming next. "I suppose you could say that," she agreed slowly.

"Why, Alyssa? Don't get me wrong, I was never more relieved in my life than I was last weekend when I woke up and found out you weren't married. But I can't help being curious. Why have you let your career keep you from having a husband and a home?"

"Jordan...I... It's difficult to explain," she murmured awkwardly.

"Try me."

There was a new, seductive tone in his voice now, not unrelated to the gentle come-hither quality his words held when he was physically seducing her, and Alyssa found it just as unsettling. She found herself wanting to respond, wanting to accept the invitation to confide, just as, in other circumstances, she found herself wanting to respond physically. What magic did this man have over her? she asked herself once again. But she heard herself struggling to explain nevertheless.

She told him about her brilliant husband and her equally brilliant father. How she'd never been able to keep up with that brilliance, try as she would.

"A lot of hard work just doesn't compensate for lack of genius," she said with a half smile. "Not in their world."

"But it does in the corporate world?" Jordan asked shrewdly.

"It seems to go much farther in the business world, yes," Alyssa agreed. "Or perhaps what abilities I have are just more appreciated in that world. Whatever the reason, I will be earning more than my father did or Chad ever will one of these days. I may not be a genius, but I will be successful. Very, very successful." Her voice grew firmer as she talked. Her successful, profitable future stretched out before her. If only she could make certain it wasn't destroyed by her reckless action in going to Vegas.

"And the gambling?" Jordan prodded gently. "Where does your new hobby fit in to your career-oriented future?"

"It doesn't." She sighed regretfully. "I should never have let myself be seduced by the fun I had."

"Or me? Do you wish you'd never let yourself be seduced by me, either, Alyssa?"

She came to a sudden halt in the sand, turning to stare up at him. She wanted to yell at him, to tell him that was exactly what she wished. But it was unexpectedly hard to look up into those questioning, golden eyes and loudly affirm her disgust or her regret. She found herself vividly, unnervingly aware of the vulnerability in his gaze as he asked the question, and somehow, in that moment, Alyssa couldn't find the willpower to tell him he had guessed correctly.

"We'd better be getting back to the house, Jordan. I promised the McGregors we'd bring a salad this afternoon." Very firmly, she started back along the beach. Obediently, Jordan fell into step beside her.

CHAPTER EIGHT

DAVID AND MILDRED MCGREGOR HAD a magnificent home in an expensive subdivision that was just off the ocean. The development had been planned so that every owner had a private boat slip, and the McGregors, Alyssa knew, had a yacht in their slip that nicely complemented the home above it.

She watched as Jordan leaned over the balcony railing and admired the beautiful boat below. David McGregor was more than happy to expound on the virtues of his prized possession, and Jordan, Alyssa had to admit, was a very complimentary listener. He was well into his role this afternoon. She felt a wry tug of amusement at the knowledge, and there was a soft smile in her eyes as she turned to help Mildred McGregor set some snacks within easy reach for the coming game of bridge.

"I'm so glad you and Jordan could make it this afternoon. I know it was awfully short notice," Mildred was saying chattily as she set out the deck of cards and the score pads. "But David had this flash of inspiration over breakfast, and I said, Why not? Go ahead and give Alyssa a call. If she and Jordan don't have anything planned, perhaps they'd like to join us!"

"It was very kind of you," Alyssa murmured, wishing privately that her boss's flash of "inspiration" had been reserved for another time. She didn't trust the way he was zeroing in on Jordan over there by the railing. Ostensibly, they were still discussing the boat, but Alyssa knew there was a subtle probing behind each casual question.

"Well, I think we're about ready," Mildred called cheerfully to the two men. "I'm really looking forward to this, you know. David and I just love bridge. We normally play at least once a week."

"Is that a warning?" Jordan grinned good-naturedly as he took a seat opposite Alyssa. "Are Alyssa and I about to get trounced by a couple of professionals?"

Alyssa closed her eyes in silent prayer. No jokes, Jordan. Please, no jokes!

"Oh, we're just friendly players, aren't we, David?" Mildred smiled brightly across the table at her husband and partner.

"That's right, my dear, just friendly," McGregor agreed as he picked up the deck of cards and began shuffling. "Jordan, here, was telling me this is his first visit to Ventura, Alyssa." He dealt the required thirteen cards per player as he spoke.

"Uh, yes. Yes, it is. At least," she added sweetly, "it's his first visit for the purpose of seeing me."

"I'm anticipating many more in the near future," Jordan drawled, his eyes gleaming in subtle amusement at her attempt to imply that their relationship was not overly intimate. "This is a beautiful stretch of coast along here."

"Will your work allow you to visit frequently?" McGregor inquired pointedly as he finished dealing the cards.

"I see no problem. It's easy enough to get a flight from Nevada, you know. And I'm counting on Alyssa wanting to come visit me occasionally, too, while I'm working there."

Alyssa flashed him a warning glance as everyone picked up his or her hand of cards. Fortunately the bidding portion of the game came next, and no one would be expected to carry on idle chatter.

It was during the bidding that Alyssa first became aware of an unexpected aspect of the game being played. She and Jordan were turning out to be natural partners. By the time the thirteen tricks had been played and the McGregors had fulfilled their contract, Alyssa was sure of it. Between them, she and Jordan had very neatly allowed the opposing team to score the opening points. As everyone started chatting again and jotting down the score, she caught Jordan's eye across the table. He smiled back blandly, but there was a hint of laughter in the golden eyes. Between the two of them, they could just as easily have conducted a strong defense, one that would have prevented the McGregors from taking the needed tricks. Playing bridge with Jordan was like playing with someone whose mind she could read and who could read hers. It was a strange and surprisingly intimate experience.

"How long have you been working for the Nevada firm, Jordan?" David McGregor inquired as the cards were collected for the next game.

Alyssa held her breath, waiting for Jordan's response.

"Not long," Jordan smiled, taking a sip from the soft drink he'd requested from Mrs. McGregor. Alyssa guessed that, out of habit, he simply didn't care to risk drinking while he was working. And playing a "friendly" game of bridge must still seem like work to him, especially since she'd given him strict instructions as to the outcome of the afternoon's game. "You know how a contract assignment is. One just does one's job and then goes on to the next assignment. I expect I'll be there a few more weeks and that will be it."

"I see," McGregor murmured as Alyssa took her turn at dealing the cards. "Then you move around a great deal in your line of work?"

Alyssa didn't like the direction of the questioning. Was McGregor fishing to see if Jordan was only a temporary fixture in her life, or was he trying to estimate the chances of her marrying Jordan and leaving Ventura to follow him on his various contract assignments? She had to make things very clear in that regard.

"Poor Jordan, always having to take off for unknown parts," she chirped breezily as she rapidly dealt the hand. "Not like me. I'm quite happy having a stable home life and friends and career. I've just fallen in love with Ventura since I moved here four years ago. I'll bet you have, too, haven't you, Mildred?"

Mildred McGregor moved unconsciously to her assistance, rhapsodizing about her work with the local museum and an artists' guild. The enthusiastic monologue carried them through the dangerous moments between games, and then, mercifully, play commenced once again.

But Jordan had not been delighted with the way Alyssa had interceded to field McGregor's question. She caught the admonishing glitter in his gaze just before he deliberately won the bidding. She knew he'd done it deliberately, and she was helpless to forestall what happened next. He took the huge number of tricks he'd contracted for, and they won the game handily. There was no way she could halt him. Since McGregor had doubled the bid, Alyssa and Jordan scored twice the number of points they would have otherwise.

The whole thing had been an object lesson for her.

If she wanted Jordan to cooperate in the final outcome of the rubber, she had damned well better let him do his own talking. He had made his point. She sent him a resentful glance, but it was met by narrowed eyes that only promised more trouble if she interfered again. If only she could have deliberately sabotaged his move, but she knew it would have been far too blatant on her part to do so. The McGregors would have wondered what in the world had gotten into her. Losing had to be done in a more subtle fashion, and in this case it took the cooperation of both partners.

The not-so-subtle probing on David McGregor's part continued as the game wore on. It was difficult giving her attention to the game and having to worry about how Jordan would handle the next question he received from McGregor. It was worse than taking a man home to meet your father, Alyssa decided disgustedly. Her boss was determined to ascertain his future plans, and Jordan insisted on making all his answers ambiguous.

Yes, he certainly traveled a great deal in his job, but no, he didn't think that was going to stop him from being able to see Alyssa frequently.

"Nothing could stop me from seeing her frequently," he murmured in a lover's smile as he glanced at the lady in question.

Alyssa seethed silently, helpless to set the record straight. It was really getting to be too much, she

decided grimly as Jordan reached for the deck of cards
to take his turn at dealing. First he had taken it upon
himself to upset her nicely structured life by showing
up on her doorstep last night, and now he was doing
his best to convince her boss that he had a continuing
role in her future.

The problem, she realized with a flash of insight,
was that he was enjoying himself while creating this
fantasy. Just as he had enjoyed himself last night.
Jordan was painting a pleasant, respectable picture of
himself, and he wasn't going to abandon the task willingly. He was having too much fun.

So he wanted to play at being domesticated, did he?

When the inevitable, direct question finally came,
it was from Mildred McGregor, not her husband, who
would probably have tried a little more subtlety.
Mildred, however, was simply curious, with a
woman's curiosity about a romance.

"Tell me, Alyssa, dear. Since it's obvious you and
Jordan are very close, when do you expect to get
married? Surely you're going to want a home with him
soon?"

Alyssa was watching Jordan's hands as he picked
up the cards and prepared to shuffle. At the word
"married," she could have sworn that his sure, confi-
dent movements faltered a fraction. Mrs. McGregor's
question had shaken her, but it was apparent that it had
had an equally unnerving affect on Jordan. Well, it was

his own fault that they were confronted with the problem, she told herself furiously. If he hadn't spent the afternoon implying a comfortable future together Mildred would never have asked the forthright question.

Very well, if the man wanted to play at being respectable, Alyssa decided in vast annoyance, she'd make him look eminently respectable!

"How very perceptive of you, Mrs. McGregor," she drawled politely, her eyes locked with Jordan's now-unreadable gaze. "Jordan and I were just discussing marriage this morning, weren't we, dear? I think Ventura would make a very nice home base for him. After all, I couldn't possibly follow him around all over the world, and I do have my work and my friends here. But marriage would give him a place to call home, too, and I think it might work out rather well."

There was a short, stunned silence from the other side of the table as Jordan began to shuffle. He wasn't looking at the cards in his hands, however, he was staring at Alyssa.

"Marriage?" he finally repeated as if the word were totally alien to him.

"Why not, darling?" she murmured, taking an enormous amount of satisfaction out of having forced him to confront the results of his fantasy playing. "Can you think of any reason why we shouldn't go ahead and tie the knot?"

There was a hissing, snapping sound as fifty-two cards went slithering across the table.

Everyone stared automatically at the confusion on the table, but only Alyssa could begin to guess how deeply shocked Jordan must have been to have lost his inevitable, perfect control. He, too, was staring, dumbfounded, at the fifty-two scattered cards as if he couldn't believe his skilled, near-magic hands had let him down in such a fashion. Alyssa could have sworn that the dark-eyed stain along the high bones of his cheeks was one of pure embarrassment.

"Excuse me," he murmured very meekly as he collected the cards. "It's been a while since I've played."

Like about two days, Alyssa thought vengefully.

McGregor chuckled jovially. "Sure it wasn't the notion of marriage which jarred you there, Jordan?" He winked at the younger man as Jordan dealt the hand with great care.

But nothing, not even a discussion of marriage, could put a professional gambler off his stride for long. Jordan dealt the last of the cards and grinned at his host in a very man-to-man fashion. "The jarring part was hearing Alyssa say it might be a good idea," he declared gently. "Do you realize how hard it is these days to convince a woman who thinks she's got everything to get married?" He shot a sudden, terrifyingly straight look at his partner. "All this time I've been wondering how to convince her, and here she is proposing to me over a game of bridge."

Alyssa drew in her breath, abruptly frightened at the results of her reckless desire to teach him a lesson. Now they were both trapped in the new fantasy. The only thing to do was play it to the hilt.

"Now that you've convinced her," David McGregor said evenly, picking up his cards, "are you going to run off with her?"

Alyssa froze. Jordan could ruin everything with his next answer. If he decided to punish her for having forced the fantasy to such an awkward conclusion, she could kiss her career good-bye. McGregor would not be interested in promoting a female who was in danger of leaving her job to follow her husband. He would consider the time spent training her an expensive waste.

She knew Jordan was aware of the tension in her; he must have seen the whiteness around her knuckles as she held the thirteen cards in her hand. Besides, he could almost read her mind, couldn't he? She waited in an agony of anxiety for him to salvage the situation.

"I would never take Alyssa away from the job she seems to love so much," Jordan said softly. "And, as she said, I need a home base, anyway. There's no reason it shouldn't be here in Ventura."

"Oh, David, isn't this lovely?" Mildred burst out happily. "Just think! We may have been instrumental in bringing about a marriage!"

"Oh, I get the feeing it was inevitable, my pet."

David smiled indulgently at his wife. "Wouldn't you say so, Jordan?"

"Inevitable," Jordan agreed dryly, and firmly began the bidding.

"Just the same," Mildred declared, unwilling to be squelched so quickly, "I think I'll break out that bottle of champagne I've been saving. It will go nicely with the steak."

Jordan's first remark a few hours later, as they finally drove home, was an exclamation of unadorned shock. "Folks in your world play rough, don't they?"

Alyssa stirred uneasily in her seat. "What do you mean?" She had been dreading the first minutes alone with him, and now they were upon her.

"I mean the way McGregor and his wife pushed you about your future plans with me. They got pretty damn personal, didn't they?"

Whatever she had been expecting from him, it wasn't this sort of remark. "I told you McGregor was going to vet you this afternoon. He's on the verge of making his promotion decision. After meeting you last night and listening to you call me 'honey' all evening, he was bound to wonder how serious we were about each other. Don't forget that crack you made to him as he was leaving last night! The one where you referred to the job of keeping an eye on your property!" The outrage was sharp in her voice.

"That wasn't nearly as bad as suggesting we get

married in front of the McGregors." Jordan grinned unrepentantly, his fine hands steady and skilled on the wheel of the Camaro he had rented. "Whatever made you say that, for God's sake?"

He didn't seem unduly upset, merely curious. Alyssa groaned. "I don't know. A lot of reasons. You were leaving such tantalizing trails for McGregor, suggesting a long-term future for us. I was getting worried that he would think we were planning on a long-range affair or something. Mildred doesn't approve of people living together, you know. And, frankly, I'm not altogether sure McGregor does, either. They're both a little on the conservative side. Besides, I figured you deserved to find yourself in a corner after the way you'd been blithely enjoying your fantasy of respectability all afternoon!"

"You decided you'd show me what respectable really means, hmmm? Okay, I can understand why you did it. But that doesn't make it right for the McGregors to put you on the spot like that. In my world, no one would dream of inquiring so pointedly into someone's background. The only thing that counts is that a person knows a little gambling etiquette and can cover his or her losses."

"Well, this isn't your world!" He was right, of course, but that was the way things were.

"No," he agreed quietly. "It's not, is it? But my first observation still holds. Folks play rough in your world."

She hadn't thought about it quite like that before. If anyone had asked her, she would have said the gambling world was far more ruthless. Now she realized she was seeing matters from a sightly different perspective because of Jordan. "Perhaps. But I have to play by the rules in my world."

"Do you? When you're in my environment, you make the rules work almost entirely in your favor."

"I don't have as much control here," she sighed. "It's different. Jordan, I'm sorry about putting us both on the spot this afternoon. I guess I was beginning to lose my temper."

He shrugged. "I'm surprised you got so carried away. After all, it would be far easier to hide the real truth about me if we were just having an affair than it would be if we got married. People are prepared to allow a certain privacy to a couple involved in an affair. If we were to get married, someone would be bound to wonder what the hell I really do for a living, and once the questions started in earnest, it would probably be impossible to stop them, wouldn't it?"

She heard the hard note in his words and felt a strange pang of uncertainty. What did he want from her? Surely he wasn't actually suggesting marriage, even obliquely? Or did his desire to live a portion of his life in her world extend that far? "Jordan? Are you….are you saying you might want to get married?" She didn't know what made her ask the question.

Alyssa only knew she couldn't seem to prevent the words from coming out. In the next instant, however, her doubts were firmly set to rest.

"No," he declared with a harshness she had never heard from him. "I'm not suggesting marriage. I've never really considered going that far with a woman, but if I did, I sure as hell would not want a wife who felt she had to hide my real occupation from all her friends and coworkers! Let's get something straight, Alyssa. I enjoy occasionally playing charades in your world, but I wouldn't want to try living them continuously. It wouldn't work. Sooner or later, as I said, the questions would get a little too pointed, and everything would fall apart."

"But you're willing to have an affair with me, is that it?" she asked tightly, aware of a sharp sense of pain and loss. Which was ridiculous. How could you lose something you never really had?

"That seems to be all that's available to me, doesn't it?" he returned dryly. "I'm sure you're no more eager to risk marrying me than I am to have a wife who's embarrassed about my background even though she sneaks out occasionally to go slumming in my neighborhood."

"That's not fair!" she retorted, stung. "You're the one who's always been so opposed to marriage! You've told me that a gambler doesn't make good husband material on more than one occasion!"

"So I have," he agreed in a suspiciously neutral tone. "So why are we arguing, hmmm? We're both agreed that marriage is extremely out of the question for us in spite of what you said when you got carried away in front of your boss this afternoon. Shall we change the subject?"

Alyssa blinked owlishly, wondering at the restlessness she was experiencing. She wanted to go on arguing about how they couldn't possibly get married, yet they were in perfect agreement on the matter, weren't they? Hadn't Jordan just said so? Damn it to hell! Why was she feeling so unsure of herself and the situation? Everything was under control. Soon Jordan would be going back to Vegas, and further downstream she would be able to tell the McGregors gently that the marriage plans with Jordan just hadn't worked out. She would tell them that, of course, after the promotion decision had been made. She wouldn't want to take the risk of having the news make a negative impact on McGregor's ultimate decision. It would be safer to wait.

Yes, she told herself determinedly, that was the real reason she would wait to make her announcement. It would be safer for her career.

"How did I do this afternoon, honey?" Jordan asked, interrupting her racing thoughts. "Did I do a good enough job of losing to satisfy you?"

She slid him a speculative glance as he parked the

Camaro in her drive. Damn it, if he wanted to change the topic, she'd show him she could do just as good a job. The discussion of their nonmarriage was definitely closed. "I thought we lost brilliantly together," she drawled.

"We did, didn't we? Could have won just as brilliantly, too," he murmured, sliding out of the front seat and slamming the door behind him. "We play rather well together."

"The McGregors enjoyed winning," she reminded him as he followed her into the house.

"Anything to please the McGregors."

She narrowed her eyes. "That was the whole point of the afternoon, Jordan," she reminded him.

"Don't look at me like that. Except for your faux pas concerning the issue of marriage, everything went perfectly." He swung around on his heel and headed for her kitchen. "I need a drink. A real drink. Didn't I see some cognac in one of these cupboards this morning? How about a glass before we go to bed?"

Bed. Alyssa stood very still in the center of her living-room floor and listened to the sound of his banging cupboard doors open and shut in the kitchen. It was late. Time to go to bed.

A frisson of sensual tension laced with feminine resistance spread through her nerve endings as she stood staring at the empty kitchen doorway. She needed time to think, Alyssa realized. She was nervous and uneasy.

The afternoon had taken more out of her than she would have guessed. Standing there now, waiting for him to reappear with the cognac, she felt the strangest desire to run and hide from him. Something had to be dealt with in her head before she could risk letting herself be seduced again by Jordan Kyle. Something vitally important.

Not understanding fully her own motivation, Alyssa glanced down the hall toward her bedroom. A part of her longed for escape behind a locked door tonight. She needed a place and time to be by herself. But in another moment Jordan would reappear in the kitchen doorway, and as soon as he touched her, she would be lost.

Without stopping to think, she turned on one heel and started toward the safety of her room. Alyssa had taken two hurried steps before his voice caught her in mid-stride.

"Going somewhere?" The dark, dangerous drawl was heavy with a sardonic tone.

She halted abruptly, her eyes closing once in quiet despair and resignation before spinning slowly to face him. Jordan stood in the kitchen doorway, one hand holding the cognac bottle and two glasses. His eyes raked coolly over her tense figure before returning to collide with her own wary, silently pleading gaze.

"Jordan, please. I…I want to sleep alone tonight," she whispered starkly, not knowing any subtle way of asking him to let her go.

He pushed himself away from the doorjamb and moved deliberately to the white overstuffed chair by the window. Flinging himself down in a careless sprawl, he poured a snifter of cognac and set the bottle on the low glass table beside him. Without a word, he lifted the snifter and took an appreciative sip. During the whole process, his eyes never left her.

Alyssa didn't know what to do. She felt trapped, unable to retreat or attack, wholly at his mercy.

"Well? What are you waiting for? Permission to go to bed? You're excused." He waved her off with one hand and took another swallow of the cognac.

"But, Jordan..." she began uncertainly. She couldn't even guess what he was thinking.

"Don't worry about me. I saw where you keep the extra blankets in the hall closet this morning. I'll sleep on your couch. Good night, Alyssa."

Anger began to simmer in her unexpectedly. How dare he be so damn casual about the situation? "What are you going to do?"

"Put a large dent in this excellent cognac," he returned readily, pouring out some more. He leaned his dark head back against the white cushion behind him and gazed at her through narrowed lids. "And then I'll go to bed. Don't worry about me, Alyssa. I've been taking care of myself for a very long time."

Yes, she thought, he had. Whirling, Alyssa fled down the hall to her room. Safe behind the shelter of her door, she sagged against it and heaved a deep sigh, which she told herself was one of relief.

When her knees had stopped trembling in reaction, she made herself begin the process of getting ready for bed. But with every move she made, every routine she went through, she found herself listening for sounds from the living room. What was Jordan doing? Was he just going to sit there and get quietly drunk? The thought made her strangely sad. The instinct to comfort surged within her as she turned back the covers and crawled into bed.

But there was no need to feel sorry for him, she scolded herself. She was the one who needed the consolation! She was the one who was facing potential disaster by allowing him to stay even one more night under her roof.

Why had he followed her? Why couldn't he have stayed in Vegas where he belonged? Dejectedly, she punched the pillow, taking out her frustration on the defenseless object. Everything would have been just fine if Jordan had kept to his world.

Or would it? How long would she have been able to conduct an affair like that, slipping back and forth between fantasy and reality? Was that what she really wanted for herself? An affair was an affair, after all, and sooner or later it ended.

That thought made her cringe a little beneath the sheet. In a blinding flash of awareness, Alyssa realized that she didn't want her affair with Jordan to ever end.

For long moments, she lay staring wide-eyed at the shadowy ceiling. But all affairs ended, and a situation as precarious as the one she was in should probably be concluded as quickly as possible. Jordan had made it clear he was not going to be content to be relegated to her fantasy life, and in all honesty, Alyssa couldn't quite convince herself she really wanted him to be. A man like Jordan moved into one's world and made himself a part of it whether or not either party wanted it that way. How could she even look at another man during the week knowing Jordan would be waiting for her on the weekends, even assuming she could bring herself to separate totally her real world from the slightly dangerous, disreputable fantasy one?

She had let herself be plunged into a reckless situation from which there was no escape now that Jordan had infiltrated her life. Having insisted on sleeping alone tonight, all she could think about was the man drinking her expensive cognac out there in her living room. She wanted Jordan in a way she had never wanted any other man. No, it was so much more than desire.

He was all wrong, a mistake on her part, a dangerous miscalculation, yet she had fallen in love with her mathematical gambler.

Alyssa lay tensely in the bed, stunned by the full

meaning of that revelation. She was in love. It shouldn't have been possible, but there was no way to deny it now that the truth had been faced. So much for the safety of sleeping alone, she thought wryly. There had been no safety at all in her whirling thoughts.

And what was she supposed to do now?

Before her restless mind could pursue that course of thought, it was diverted by the soft, sure sound of the bedroom door being opened. The shiver of fear and sensual tension she had experienced earlier went through her once more. Alyssa didn't stir. In that moment, she didn't think she could have moved so much as an inch.

From her half-curled position on the bed, she watched the shaft of light from the opening door as it widened and spread out on the carpet, seeking her. Through nearly closed eyes, she waited tautly for whatever was to happen next.

Jordan's lean, dark form filled the doorway. The light was behind him, and she could not read the expression on his face, but she sensed the male power in him—an ancient plea and an equally ancient demand.

"I have discovered," he said very quietly and too distinctly, "that I do not care for drinking alone."

Alyssa held her breath. Was he awfully drunk? How much time had passed since he'd slung himself down into that chair and started pouring cognac? How much time had she lain there coming to the shattering conclusion that she was in love?

He came gliding silently across the carpet toward the bed and halted to stand beside it, gazing down at her still form. "I have also discovered that I do not care for sleeping alone when the woman who belongs to me is only a few steps away."

Alyssa found her voice, although it proved only a breathless whisper. "Are you very sure that I belong to you, Jordan?" Why did so much seem to ride on his answer?

He watched her broodingly, his golden eyes the only visible features of his face. Even they were shadowed and unreadable in the pale light. "Do you doubt it?" he countered softly.

"Oh, Jordan, no. Not tonight." Alyssa put out a hand, and an instant later her fingers were seized in the warm manacle of his sure, enthralling grip.

"I didn't think you could, Alyssa. I knew you were tense after what happened during the bridge game, but I didn't think you could go on denying me all night long." The words were a husky groan of desire and satisfaction.

He came down beside her and gathered her into his arms, his hands possessive and seeking on her body, and Alyssa gave herself up to the magic with a soft sigh. This was the man who could read her mind. Hadn't she learned that much during the bridge game? He seemed to know her body and her mind the way he knew numbers and cards and dice.

It was dangerous for a woman to give herself to a man who knew her so intimately. But it was also irresistible.

On Monday morning, when she returned to work and her gambler returned to Las Vegas, Alyssa promised herself, she would sort out the reckless tangle she had created by trying to weave reality and fantasy together.

CHAPTER NINE

MONDAY BROUGHT WITH IT NO GREAT improvement in the clarity of her thinking, however. Alyssa felt as though she wandered through the day in a haze, performing her duties, dealing with coworkers and clients and generally acting with some semblance of normality.

But she didn't feel normal. She hadn't felt anything approaching that condition since Saturday night when she had acknowledged the truth of her feelings about Jordan.

Thinking back to those unnerving moments as she sat at her desk, Alyssa automatically reached for the sheet of paper that she had found on Sunday after Jordan had kissed her good-by and started out for the airport. When she had discovered the paper, half hidden under the white chair where he had sat drinking cognac, Alyssa had realized how he had been occupying his thoughts that night after the bridge game.

He had been drawing Pascal's triangle. The rows of numbers in the shape of a triangle were a simple, classic aid to calculating probabilities. Each number in the table was the sum of the two numbers above it. Had Jordan sprawled in the chair that night trying to sort out his own thoughts by concentrating on the clear, utterly logical progression of numbers? A tiny smile edged her lips as Alyssa considered the image that presented. Jordan had spent a long time drinking cognac and playing with math in an attempt to keep from coming to her bed, and in the end he had failed.

Carefully, she refolded the sheet of paper. Some women took out pictures of their lovers and gazed at them fondly. She had only a sample of his math to look at until next weekend when she boarded the plane for Las Vegas.

He had made her promise to return to the gambling city just before he had climbed into the rented Camaro.

"I have work to do," he'd said, smiling wryly at he stood beside the car and framed her face with rough palms. "It may not be particularly respectable work, but it pays well, and I have to get back to it. You'll be on the Friday-night flight this time? No unexpected prior commitments?"

"I'll be on the flight," she'd promised, looking up at him with eyes that glittered with a suspicious dampness. She loved the man and didn't know quite how to tell him. She wasn't even sure he'd want such a confession from her. All Jordan had demanded and received was the admission that she belonged to him.

Sooner or later, Alyssa thought as she pushed the paper with Pascal's triangle on it into her purse, they would have to arrive at some reasonable way of handling the passion that existed between them. How long would it be safe to conduct an affair? How long before the truth came out and shattered her carefully structured world? What would she do when the inevitable moment arrived?

Time enough to worry about it when it happened, Alyssa told herself, picking up a desk-top calculator and going back to work. She would deal with the situation when it occurred. In the meantime, there was no reason not to have the best of both worlds, was there? And there was another possibility....

She thought again of the mathematical work on the sheet of paper. Jordan was good. He not only had natural ability; he'd taken enough formal classes from time to time to learn about things like Pascal's triangle. On Sunday afternoon, she'd discovered him pouring over one of her textbooks on probability, and when she'd said something about one of the theorems in it, she'd been surprised to discover that he knew all about it.

His math might have heavily slanted toward gambling applications, but he had ability and some general knowledge. What if she got him a job? A real job? What if she made him truly respectable. Would he consider marriage?

That tantalizing thought was interrupted as Hugh Davis sauntered into her office. Warily, Alyssa put away her dreams and focused her whole attention on her arch rival. Since the night of the party, she had trusted him even less than she had in the past.

"Have a pleasant weekend, Alyssa?" he drawled smoothly, sitting down without waiting to be asked.

"Yes, thank you. And yourself?" She leaned back in her swivel chair, tapping the end of a pencil on the polished desk top in a small, almost concealed gesture of impatience.

"An interesting weekend. Very interesting." He laced his fingers together and smiled at her the way a predator smiles at a victim. "My wife cried a lot after your party."

More uneasy than ever, Alyssa frowned. "I'd say that was your own fault. You shouldn't have made it look as if you were flirting with me."

"Ah, yes. Well, you see it wasn't just what she thought she saw at the party," he murmured. "She had a lot of other evidence to go on, too."

Alyssa stared at him. "What the devil are you talking about?" she gasped.

"I'm talking about the way I've been letting her think I'm having an affair with you," Hugh said indifferently.

"My God! Hugh, why would you do such a thing?"

"To protect the woman with whom I actually am

having an affair, naturally." He shrugged as if it were the most natural thing in the world. "I deliberately established a few false trails. You were very helpful, by the way, being gone almost every weekend for a couple of months. Very often you would casually mention you were going to be 'out of town' whenever I asked you what you had planned for the weekends, remember?"

Appalled, she stared at him. She had usually mentioned leaving town because she didn't want him thinking of an excuse to drop by. She'd been trying to protect herself, and all the while he'd been using her!

"Don't look so stunned, Alyssa. You would have been relatively safe if my wife hadn't gone to unexpected lengths to find out what the two of us were up to on the weekends. You see, I've been gone a lot, also."

"Hugh, so help me, if you don't explain what the hell you think you're trying to do…!"

"My wife is a very possessive woman, but she has an interesting characteristic. She tends to blame the 'other woman' whenever I have an affair. Some nonsense about how I was lured away from hearth and home. Some psychological twist, I expect. By not blaming me, she hasn't had to deal with me, if you see what I mean. She only has to deal with the other woman. Naturally, I didn't want her dealing with the real woman, so I made use of your frequent absences to cover my own. It's been extremely convenient for protecting my, er, friend."

"I can imagine," she said furiously. "So every weekend I've been gone, your poor wife has assumed you were with me, is that it?"

"That's it. You don't have to worry. I've told her it's all over between us."

Alyssa remembered the phone calls during the previous week, the ones when there had only been silence on the other end of the line after she'd answered. Cari Davis checking up on her? Probably.

"Why are you telling me this now, Hugh?" she demanded stonily.

"Because my wife went above and beyond her usual efforts this time, as I discovered the night of your party. You, my dear, were such a threat to her that she actually employed a private detective to follow you on a couple of recent weekends. The private eye informed her that you were definitely not with me. In the course of his report, he mentioned where you had been spending your time. You apparently have developed a fatal compulsion of late, Alyssa, haven't you?"

She didn't move, every nerve and fiber of her being rock still as the full impact of what was happening came home to her. Alyssa waited.

"When I found out Friday night exactly what my wife had discovered in the course of her latest 'research,' I made her tell me the name of the investigator she had employed, and yesterday morning I tracked him down and told him he was now working for me."

"And your wife?" Alyssa could hardly breathe.

"Up until Friday night," he mocked, "she refused to believe she'd gotten her money's worth from the investigator. She was still convinced I must be having an affair with you. The only thing that saved you from one of her screaming confrontations with the 'other woman' was Kyle's presence. She couldn't quite figure out where he fit in and was confused enough to avoid accusing you outright at your own party. She often does things like that after she's had a few drinks. But that's really not our problem at the moment. Cari eventually will believe whatever I tell her because she doesn't want to lose me. No, you and I have no need to concern ourselves with her rather muddled thinking processes. If she'd been thinking straight, after all, she would have had the detective follow *me* these past couple of weekends," he said with a chuckle.

"But she didn't," Alyssa whispered.

"No, she didn't. And when I had interviewed the investigator, I knew I had learned some very rewarding information for which I must thank my dear wife someday. He just phoned an hour ago to tell me he'd tracked your Jordan Kyle to one of the biggest casino hotels in Vegas and had seen him check in. Kyle didn't report to any research firm in the middle of the desert, did he Alyssa? He spent Sunday night in a casino and slept late this morning. Furthermore, he showed no signs of preparing to go back to a real job. Not the kind of job he said he'd be returning to when he spoke of it Saturday night. Kyle's just some gambler you picked up on your last trip to Vegas, isn't he, Alyssa?"

"You're out of your mind!" she hissed.

"How many weekends have you spent there during the past few months? How much money have you lost? No one wins in Vegas, not in the long run. What's the matter, Alyssa, can't you stop? I hear it's like that. A compulsion that grows on you."

"You haven't got the faintest idea of what you're talking about!"

"No? I think David McGregor might appreciate my ideas."

"I see," she said tightly, understanding now exactly what was coming.

"However, I'm willing to keep the information I've uncovered to myself under certain circumstances," Hugh went on blandly.

"And what exactly would those circumstances be?" she inquired almost curiously.

"That you tell McGregor you no longer wish to be considered for the managerial slot he's got open." Hugh was abruptly on his feet, smiling evilly as he headed for the door. "I know, I know. It's blackmail. But we all do what we have to in this world. I'll stop by your house later this evening for your answer. This time my wife really will have cause to believe it's you I'm visiting, won't she?"

Numb with shock and a mounting horror, Alyssa watched him walk out her door. The end of her short-lived attempt to conduct both a fantasy life and a normal one had come with totally unexpected suddenness. Everything she had been working for had just collapsed around her. And all because she hadn't made herself resist the fun and excitement of her make-believe world.

Jordan's words came back to her: *"Folks in your world play rough, don't they?"* Somehow his world seemed much more honest and reliable than her own.

With an unnatural calm, Alyssa drove home a little early from the office. What did it matter if she broke the rules today? She was still feeling abnormally calm when she let herself in the front door of her beach-front home and dropped her purse on the nearest chair. Then she went to pour herself a stiff drink. If ever a woman needed one, it was she tonight.

Very carefully, moving as if she were walking on eggs, she crossed the living room to sink down on the chair beside the phone. For a long time, she simply stared at the instrument. What were the odds of finding Jordan in his room at this hour? Possibly rather high, she told herself coolly. He might be dressing for dinner.

But what would she say to him? How did you tell your lover you were being blackmailed? No, that wasn't the hard part. The hard part would be trying to describe the fact that she wasn't at all sure she cared.

Alyssa licked her lips and took a delicate swallow of the drink she had fixed. She wasn't sure she cared. In some ways, it was almost a relief. The inevitable ending had arrived. She was free. *Free!*

Good lord! What was she saying? Her world was collapsing around her. How could she think of herself as being freed? She shook her head uncomprehendingly, knowing she needed to talk to someone, and that someone had to be Jordan. He was the one she now turned to instinctively. In his magic hands, she would be safe.

Her nerveless fingers dialed the telephone with careful precision. She was fully prepared to have the instrument ring endlessly in an empty hotel room, so when Jordan's voice came on the other end of the line, she was startled.

"Jordan?" she whispered.

"Alyssa? What's wrong? Honey, what's happening?" The dark, rich voice was heavy with immediate concern, and Alyssa found herself responding to it unthinkingly.

"I had an interesting visit from Hugh Davis this afternoon, Jordan," she began quietly. "Did I ever tell you the man's a bastard?"

"I figured it out for myself the first time I met him," Jordan replied impatiently. "What the hell is going on?"

So she told him, slowly and distinctly, exactly what had transpired that day in her office, but he interrupted her before she got to the final part, the part about not really caring that everything was over and that she was free. Alyssa never got the chance to tell him that because he was already giving her instructions.

"It's only four-thirty," he rasped into the phone when he'd heard her tale. "I'll catch the late-afternoon flight back to L.A. It will take me about an hour and a half to drive to Ventura. If Davis gets there before I do, I want you to stall him, do you understand? Keep him talking until I arrive. Don't worry, Alyssa, I'll undo the damage I've done."

He hung up the phone before she could tell him she wasn't at all sure she wanted the damage undone and that, in any case, it wasn't his fault. He had just gotten entangled in her fantasy.

In the end, the two men arrived almost simultaneously. Hugh Davis had just knocked on Alyssa's door shortly before eight-thirty that night when there was the sound of another car crunching in the drive.

"He's not going to be any help, Alyssa," Hugh informed her, glancing back over his shoulder. "He's nothing but a professional gambler."

Jordan was so much more than that, Alyssa thought,

relief flooding through her as her lover climbed out of the car and started toward the steps to her front door. He was the man she loved.

"Jordan!" Unhesitatingly, she flew down the steps and threw herself into his arms. He took the shock of her impact without flinching, strong arms going around her and sensitive fingers instantly finding the soothing places along her spine. "Oh, Jordan, you didn't have to come all this way for me."

She felt him drop the lightest of kisses into her auburn hair as she buried her face against his solid chest. " Of course, I did, sweetheart. You belong to me, remember? I have the right to take care of you."

"Well, well, this is really a touching little scene. Who would have thought Alyssa would have been so silly as to fall for someone like you, Kyle? But I suppose there's no accounting for taste."

Slowly, Jordan freed himself from Alyssa's clinging embrace, tucking her against his side as he started toward the man waiting on the doorstep. Alyssa could feel the cool rage in him and wondered at it. All that emotion on her behalf? He must feel something very strong for her. Surely he did!

But his voice was remote and dangerous, soft with a menace that was totally controlled and all the more frightening because of it. "Let's go inside, Davis. I think we can get this little fiasco cleared up rather quickly."

Alyssa slanted Jordan a questioning glance as they mounted the steps and walked past the other man into her living room. But she could read nothing on his impassive face. Only the golden eyes were alive with a fire that threatened to consume. In that moment, she was eternally grateful that his anger was aimed at Hugh and not herself. The intensity of that anger would live in her memory for the rest of her life. What had she unleashed by dragging Jordan into this mess?

When she looked across at Hugh Davis, who stood facing them, she realized the effect was not lost on her tormentor. For the first time since she had met him, there was something besides derision in his expression. Confronting the devil with the golden eyes, Davis was learning the meaning of having taken on more than he could handle.

"This needn't concern you, Kyle," he tried, apparently having decided to take the offensive. "This is a little business matter between myself and Alyssa."

"Everything that affects Alyssa concerns me, Davis. It's too bad you didn't realize that earlier."

"All I'm offering to do is keep quiet about her new, uh, problem. She's obviously unqualified for the promotion, and if she'll take herself out of the running, I'll keep silent about the true facts. That's simple enough."

"Blackmail usually is," Jordan observed, gently releasing Alyssa and pushing her tenderly in the direction of the nearest chair. "Getting rid of black-mailers, however, is even simpler."

Davis narrowed his eyes, and his tone became blus-tering. "Going to threaten me, Kyle? If you do, I'll go to the cops, and then this whole thing really will be out in the open. Alyssa not only won't stand a chance of promotion, she won't even be able to keep the job she has!"

"I'm not threatening you," Jordan murmured, sitting down on one of the stools in front of the small eating bar. He hooked one booted heel over a rung. Dressed in a pair of charcoal slacks and an open-throated black silk shirt, he seemed very dark and dan-gerous. A golden-eyed devil, Alyssa thought once again as she watched him intently. "I'll save the threats until after we see whether or not you're capable of a bit of reason."

"What the hell's that supposed to mean?" Davis demanded. It was becoming increasingly clear that he was out of his depth. Threatening Alyssa in her office had been one thing. Dealing with Jordan Kyle was proving to be quite another.

"So you were using my woman to shield one of your own, is that it?" Jordan pursued mildly. When Davis said nothing, he nodded. "Very commendable, in a way. I approve of a man trying to protect his woman even if I don't approve of the way he does it."

"So help me, Kyle, if you don't shut up and get out

of here, I'll make sure Alyssa loses her job! Who the hell are you to interfere? You're nothing but a two-bit gambler!"

"Exactly." Jordan smiled grimly as Alyssa stirred angrily in her chair. "No, he's quite right, honey. I am a gambler. But there seems to be something our noble blackmailer has overlooked about the members of my profession."

"Such as?" Davis challenged with a sneer.

"Such as the fact that we know how to take calculated risks. We depend for survival on a lot of talents, Davis. Among those is the ability to size up a man very quickly. When I met you Saturday night, I knew almost immediately what kind of bastard you really are. One of these days, I suppose your wife will finally realize it, too. But in the meantime, suffice it to say that you, Hugh Davis, are no gentleman."

Davis gave a crack of nervous laugher at the mild observation. "I don't see how that's any handicap!"

"Perhaps, perhaps not. Having accepted that basic tenet, however, we are led to a further observation. Only a true gentleman would go out of his way to protect his woman." There was a pause while Jordan let the implication sink in. "You, not being a gentleman, couldn't be expected to really take pains to protect a woman, any woman, could you? You would only be concerned about protecting yourself in any given circumstance."

Alyssa swallowed as it dawned on her exactly where Jordan was going with his strange comments. Of course, she thought belatedly, she should have seen the flaw in Davis's strategy from the first. Why would he have used her to protect another woman? It wasn't his style to worry about someone else getting into trouble. Apparently, his wife had hounded several of his previous lovers, and it hadn't seemed to bother him. Davis was not a gentleman in any sense of the word.

"I don't know what you're getting at, Kyle," the other man snapped forcefully.

"No? I thought it was obvious." Jordan held up the well-shaped fingers of his left hand and carefully ticked off facts. "One, we have all agreed you're a bastard who wouldn't worry unduly about any woman with whom he was having an affair unless—"

"Unless?" Alyssa prompted expectantly.

"Unless," Jordan continued obligingly, holding up a second finger, "discovery of the real identity of the other woman could do Davis, here, a great deal of harm."

And then it seemed to Alyssa that all hell broke loose in her living room. Jordan suddenly flew into motion, catching an astonished Hugh by the collar of his shirt and slamming him up against the wall. "What am I going to find out about this mystery woman whose identity you've been protecting?" he growled, his face inches from the other man's now. "What will I get back in the report I'm going to request from the private investigator I'll hire tonight, Davis? *Who is she?*"

Apparently, Hugh Davis had the sense to realize when the odds were overwhelmingly against him. "It's none of your business," he said hoarsely. "For God's sake, let me go! I won't tell McGregor about you or Alyssa; just let me go!"

"The problem in dealing with a man who is definitely not a gentleman," Jordan grated, "is that one just can't trust the bastard."

"I give you my word! I won't tell McGregor!"

"I think I'll go ahead and hire my own investigator this evening. I know a very good man in L.A. He's played cards with me on occasion, in fact. I can trust him."

"Damn it, I gave you my word I'd keep quiet about Alyssa. What the hell more do you want?"

"The full truth." Jordan waited, implacable and frightening, even to Alyssa, whom he was in the process of defending. "I'll get it one way or another. Either from you tonight or from the investigator within a day or two. The only deal I'll make with you is that if you save me the trouble of hiring my friend in L.A., I'll have Alyssa keep quiet about the identity of the woman. In other words, we'll swap information, Davis. And then we'll both agree to keep silent about what we know. It's called a standoff, I think."

In the end, Davis told them. It was Alyssa who understood the full significance of the name, however. "Marilyn Crawford? You've been seeing Marilyn Crawford, Hugh?" She gasped in amazement.

There was silence from the other man as he made a show of straightening his clothing. Jordan had released the now-sullen man when he'd produced the name.

"Who is she?" Jordan asked, turning to Alyssa curiously.

"She's the president of a rival firm. No wonder Hugh wanted to keep the name to himself. McGregor would be furious if he found out one of his employees was seeing her. Yeoman Research and Marilyn Crawford's company are arch enemies. We fight over the same contracts and bid for the same projects. Marilyn's father, I understand, hated David McGregor, and when he left the firm to his daughter, he apparently left the legacy of hatred. McGregor would say without hesitation that any involvement between Hugh and Ms. Crawford clearly amounted to a conflict of interest. He's probably suspect him of selling information."

"That's not true!" Hugh blazed with surprising fury. "I wouldn't tell that bitch a damn thing!"

Jordan arched a derisive eyebrow. "Like I said. Not much of a gentleman, are you? You're calling your lover a bitch?"

"Everything's over between us," Hugh muttered tensely. "She lied to me. Promised me a position if things didn't work out at Yeoman…" He stopped, realizing he was saying too much, but Jordan merely nodded.

"So she was trying to get information out of you, and when she got what she wanted, she dropped you."

"She didn't get what she wanted!" Hugh exclaimed with such intensity that Alyssa, for one, believed him. "I never told her a damn thing about Yeoman."

"And *that's* when she decided to drop you?" Alyssa hazarded.

"We had it out yesterday. She made it very clear she was only trying to get information out of me."

"Why did you ever get involved with her, Hugh?" Alyssa asked very gently. "I know she's quite beautiful, but you must have known what McGregor would do if he ever found out."

"He'd do the same thing he'd do if he ever found out about your gambling and who Kyle, here, really is, wouldn't he?" Hugh shot back.

Alyssa winced. "Point taken. But I can tell you why I started gambling. I like it. And I don't lose any more than I can afford," she tacked on carefully, knowing he'd never believe her if she claimed that she routinely won.

Hugh lifted one shoulder with a touch of bravado. "Maybe I started seeing Marilyn for the same reasons.

She was exciting, a little dangerous, and I...I thought that if I ever were to learn anything useful from her, I might be able to use it to impress McGregor. Then she offered me a position if I didn't get this promotion. I was grateful. I still wanted the promotion, but it was nice to know there would be somewhere else to go just in case. Then, yesterday, I guess she decided her own scheme wasn't going to work, and she told me it was all over. Told me to go to hell, in fact," he added roughly.

"And suddenly getting the promotion became more important than ever, didn't it?" Alyssa concluded perceptively. "So, armed with the information your wife had accidentally dug up, you came to see me."

Hugh said nothing, his sullen glance sliding resentfully to Jordan, who smiled very blandly. "Don't ever come to see my woman again, Davis. If you try to do anything more than say hello to her in the hall at work, I'll slaughter you. And if word of Alyssa's 'hobby' ever gets out, I'll know where to come looking for the culprit, won't I?"

"You've got a deal," Hugh growled, heading for the door. "Alyssa and I will both agree to keep our mouths shut, won't we, Alyssa?" But her answer froze his fingers to the doorknob.

"You don't have to worry, you know, Hugh. The promotion is yours."

Jordan, who had been watching his victim leave,

swung around to stare at her. She smiled serenely at him, ignoring the startled Hugh. "I'm taking myself out of the running for that management post."

"What the hell…?"

"The devil you are!"

She wasn't sure which man spoke first, but her eyes never left Jordan's. "I've decided I don't really care for the lovely career I've built. Folks in this world play a little too rough for me. I want out."

"Alyssa!" Jordan reached for her, yanking her up in front of him. "Honey, you can't do this! Think about what you're saying!"

She smiled again and nodded dismissively at Hugh. "Good night, Hugh. This next part is between Jordan and myself."

Jordan shot the other man a look of warning. "You're not to say a damn thing about this, understand? Alyssa doesn't know what she's saying tonight. She will undoubtedly change her mind by morning!"

Hugh nodded, eyeing his coworker narrowly, and slammed out the door. Jordan instantly turned back to Alyssa, his powerful, supple fingers digging into her upper arms as he glared at her.

"Honey, you've been under a lot of pressure today. Don't make any hasty decisions tonight. This is your future we're talking about!"

"I know." She smiled.

"You can't just shelve it like that! You've explained to me how much it means to you."

"It meant a lot because there was no other future which sounded more appealing, and I thought I had to prove something to a couple of people whose opinions no longer matter." Her father was dead, and she had never really loved her ex-husband. She had her own life to lead.

He groaned and pulled her tightly against him. "Sweetheart, listen to me before you do anything rash. I know my world looks glamorous and exciting to you, but believe me, you wouldn't like it on a permanent basis. Hell, *I* don't particularly like it on a permanent basis! I can't let you give up everything to come and join me there. Why the hell do you think I moved heaven and earth to get here tonight in time to get you out of the trouble I'd gotten you into?"

She moved her head once in a negative gesture against his chest. "You didn't get me into trouble. I got myself into it very nicely, thank you. You were something of an innocent victim, actually."

"Alyssa, Alyssa," he crooned hoarsely, holding her so tightly she could hardly breathe. "Honey, please don't act hastily. I don't want you to regret anything. I can handle Davis if he makes more trouble."

"I'm sure you can. You handled him very well tonight. Whatever made you guess he had something to hide?"

"I wasn't absolutely sure, but it was worth a chance. There had to be some reason why he was using you as a shield. An affair is an affair. If he didn't care about his wife finding out, why hide behind the wrong woman? I gambled that there must be more to the story than what he claimed."

"And you won. As usual. You can be a little frightening, Jordan. My world isn't the only one where folks play rough, is it?"

"Don't ever be afraid of me," he groaned into her hair.

"No," she agreed gently.

"Sweetheart, I meant what I said. Please don't do anything rash like quitting your job."

"Afraid of having to support me?" she said, chuckling into his shirt.

He shook her in soft punishment. "You know damn well that's got nothing to do with it. I'm willing to support you for the rest of your life. And protect you and make love to you!"

"That's nice. Remember that when I show up in Las Vegas tomorrow night, okay?"

He held her slightly away from him, lifting her chin so that she met his searching gaze. "One more time, Alyssa. Don't act hastily. We're two intelligent, quick-thinking people. We can go on juggling both worlds together indefinitely."

"But I don't want to do that, Jordan." She pulled

free of his arms. "Would you like a glass of cognac before we go to bed?" she asked, her eyes smiling at him.

"No."

"No cognac?"

"No bed. I'm going back to Vegas tonight," he declared grimly.

"Oh, Jordan." She sighed, knowing what he was doing now because she could almost read his mind.

"I have to give you time to think," he declared, running a hand through his dark hair in exasperation. "I know that between the two of us we can make each other believe anything we want by morning."

"Which is a polite way of saying you can seduce me into forgetting everything when I'm in your arms? That I can't possibly think straight while you're making love to me?" she teased tenderly.

He shot her a narrow glance. "It works both ways, you know. Why do you think I had to come looking for you when you sent that message saying you couldn't make the Friday-night flight last week? I couldn't even pay attention to my work! All I could think about was you."

Try to understand what that means, Jordan, Alyssa pleaded silently. Try to understand that maybe that means you're in love with me the way I'm in love with you! Aloud she said persuasively, "It's a long trip back to Vegas tonight."

"Not as long as the trip getting here," he assured her grimly. "The thought of you tangling with Davis made me so damn furious I thought I'd go out of my head!"

"I tried to tell you it wasn't necessary to come and protect me, but you hung up the phone before I could get the words out."

"Believe me, it was necessary in spite of whatever you decide to do about your job tomorrow." He stood staring at her, and the helpless, vulnerable expression on his hard face made Alyssa want to cradle him in her arms and soothe him.

But there was nothing she could do at the moment. Instead, her eyes were full of her love as she said simply, "Good night, Jordan. I'll find you at the casino. I'll be arriving sometime between seven and eight, I imagine."

His mouth tightened as he read the determination in her, and he stepped forward, catching her possessively in his arms and kissing her hard. Then he was gone into the night.

CHAPTER TEN

THE FOLLOWING EVENING, ALYSSA drifted into the glittering casino sheathed in the black gown with the silver edging that she had worn the night she had met Jordan. She was every inch the sophisticated worldly lady gambler, a graceful figure of feminine mystery. Her rich auburn hair gleamed in the light of the heavy chandeliers, and the silver trim on her gown moved as if it were molten.

In the depths of her sea-colored eyes, there was a beckoning and a longing and a promise that caught the attention of more than one male as she moved through the boisterous crowd. But each seemed to take one glance and recognize that the expression wasn't meant for him. A few turned their heads, curious to see which man would claim the promise in her.

Alyssa was unaware of the reaction. She was scanning the crowd of elegantly dressed players searching for only one face. Tonight none of the glitter or the brash luxury surrounding her appealed. Tonight nothing mattered except finding the man for whom she searched. It occurred to her as she made her way through the casino that she had never felt so free before in her life.

Always there had been a predetermined goal, an end set for her by others. Her father had set impossibly high scholastic standards, hoping he had sired a genius to take his place. Her ex-husband had set her to work, luring her into marriage with the promise that somehow she could share the academic world through him, even though she wasn't quite up to the genius levels required to participate fully.

When she had finally gone out on her own, the goal of success in the business world had, in a sense, been predetermined for her, also. It was the only route left to her by which she could prove herself.

The fantasy world of the casino had been her escape for a while, but tonight she entered it knowing she no longer needed it. Tonight she had come to free not only herself but the man she loved. Together they would build a new world all their own. If he loved her, too.

That was the only hitch, of course, Alyssa reminded herself as she wound her way into the crowd, heading for the blackjack tables. Did Jordan truly love her? She was betting everything on the hope that he did. Never had the stakes been so high.

She found him seated at a blackjack table, and for a long moment she stood silently watching him as he played. Dressed in the black and white of formal evening clothes, his lean, hard body made a subtly dangerous statement. The overhead light gleamed off the Vandyke-brown hair that touched the crisp white collar of his shirt, and she knew when he turned around that the familiar golden eyes would be warm with their own inner fire. Standing very still a little distance away, she watched the smooth, sure movements of his long fingers as they placed bets and checked cards. Magic hands.

He didn't turn around until the play had ended. Then he politely accepted his modest winnings and slid off the stool, starting toward her as if he had known she was there all along. He stopped a couple of feet away, eyes raking over her, from the black patent leather sandals to the crown of her auburn head. He had known she was there, watching him, she realized because he could almost read her mind. And she could almost read his.

Almost. That was the factor that made the next step so risky. Almost was not for sure.

"Can I buy you a drink?" she murmured, knowing her outward composure probably hid the way her pulses were racing.

He smiled, remembering, as she had, the way he had approached her that first night. "It's all right," she went on, eyes glinting with a trace of laughter, "I don't work for the casino."

"No?" he questioned, coming closer by a pace as if drawn by invisible cords. The sound of his deep voice touched every nerve in her body.

"No," she assured him softly. "It's quite safe to come and have a drink with me."

"I'm not so sure about that," he said as he allowed her to take his arm and they headed toward the nearest lounge. "You look a little dangerous to me tonight."

"But I don't work for the casino. I don't work for anyone, as a matter of fact." She felt his arm tense under her fingers. "That's one of the things I wanted to speak to you about," she went on bravely. "I resigned my job today."

He seated her carefully and slid into the black leather booth beside her, his face intense. "You don't have to worry. I'll take care of you. Always."

Her mouth crooked lovingly. "That's very generous of you, but it's not quite what I had in mind."

He touched her wrist as it lay on the small table they shared, and Alyssa stirred faintly when the familiar thrill trickled through her. "What, exactly, did you have in mind?" he murmured. He was looking at her, she suddenly realized, as if he couldn't quite believe she was there. Had he really thought that in the end she would choose her job and her world instead of him?

"I had in mind a new career for both of us, Jordan.

Something quite respectable. You seem to be lured by the prospect of respectability." Alyssa held her breath after she made the statement. Would he want what she was going to suggest?

The fingers on her wrist ceased their gentle tracing. "What are you suggesting?"

"A consulting firm with a name like Chandler-Kyle. Or, if you insist, Kyle-Chandler. A firm which would offer statistical and probability consulting to business. One that would not get involved in government contracts where a reckless past might prove a hindrance. We would have to invest in some hardware, like a computer, and some of your skills might have to be expanded a bit in new directions, but on the whole I think that, between us, we have a lot of potential."

"And if it didn't work out?"

"Then we could always fall back on making our living by our wits, couldn't we?" she murmured, flicking a careless hand toward the active casino floor in front of them. "In fact, we might find gambling a useful way to drum up a little capital for our new business. We might also find it a pleasant way to spend our vacations."

"In other words, you're suggesting we make a stab at having the best of both worlds?"

"On our own terms. Which we can do if we don't

work for other people who have prejudices against our particular talents."

His fingers began to move again, drawing an intimate design on the vulnerable skin of her palm. His eyes never left her face. "Do you think I could hold up my end of such a consulting firm?"

So that was it. Lacking the formal degrees, Jordan apparently lacked some confidence in his own abilities. Alyssa didn't. "I've been around enough mathematicians in my life to know true ability when I see it. Believe me, Jordan, you've got it. You may not have a degree, but you seem to have acquired a formidable amount of training along the way. Between us we have the skills."

He drew in his breath. "The skills to be respectable."

"Yes." Damn it, what was he thinking? All at once, Alyssa couldn't read even a fraction of his mind. The heat in his eyes was almost overwhelming, however, and she tried to take heart from it.

"And on our own we can still wander in and out of your fantasy on occasion?" he pursued thoughtfully.

"If you like," she amended cautiously.

Then he smiled, a brilliant, challenging grin that set all her fears to rest in one fell swoop. "Oh, I think I'd like that. This world of mine might be a hell of a lot more fun once I knew I wasn't trapped in it. You've got yourself a deal, Alyssa Chandler. We'll toss a coin to see whether the new firm's name will be Chandler-Kyle or Kyle-Chandler."

"If you don't mind, I'd like to be the one who does the tossing," she murmured.

He threw back his head with a laugh that drew several interested stares. "Don't you trust me, sweetheart?"

"With my life," she responded immediately.

"Oh, Alyssa!" Then he was pulling her hard against him, finding her mouth with his own in a kiss that swirled her helplessly into a loving, sensual world full of promise and hope and commitment. His mouth moved on hers, draining every vestige of uncertainty from her and replacing it with sureness and spinning wonder. "Alyssa" —he breathed raggedly when he reluctantly lifted his head— "Alyssa, my sweet lady gambler. If you're willing to take a chance on me, I swear I'll never let you down. I'll give you everything I have to give."

She swallowed and took the final risk. "Your love, Jordan? Could you give me a little of your love?"

He shuddered, his eyes almost tortured. "My God! Don't you know you've had that from the first?"

"Jordan"—she sighed, leaning her head down on his shoulder—"oh, Jordan. Have I really? I love you so very much, you know…"

"I was beginning to hope you might when you talked of quitting your job last night, but I was almost afraid to start counting on it," he confessed huskily.

"I didn't think you were afraid to count on anything," she taunted gently. "After all, you count so well!"

"Some things, unfortunately, are true risks. Real gambles. They're a bit scary. Alyssa, if you really love me—"

"You know I do." She lifted glowing eyes to meet his shattering gaze. She could have sworn that he moistened his lips with the tip of his tongue, as if he were actually nervous.

"Then as long as you're proposing to make a respectable man out of me, I'm going to propose that I return the favor."

"Make a respectable woman out of me?"

"Will you marry me, Alyssa?"

She caught her breath, her heart in her throat. "You…you always said you weren't good husband material."

"I am now," he retorted confidently, even a little arrogantly, as if he were suddenly very sure of himself. "Marry me, Alyssa, and you can bet I'll make the best damned husband material around!"

"It's a deal," she whispered.

JORDAN FLATLY REFUSED TO EVEN consider a Las Vegas wedding. And although Alyssa pointed out that if they got married there they would be able to spend their honeymoon in the bordello-red bedroom suite, he refused to reconsider. If they were going to be respectable, he declared, they were going to start off on the right foot. A quiet wedding with a real minister. He produced both in the small town of Oregon where he had his house on the coast.

"Nice car," Alyssa observed politely as he drove her home from the minister's three days after he had swept her out of the casino and off to Oregon.

Jordan winced as he handled the wheel of the silver Porsche. "I forgot you told me that first night you were going to use your gambling winnings on a red Porsche. Well, don't worry, sweetheart. I'll buy you one."

She chuckled. "I don't think we need two in the family. I'll just use yours. Unless," she added blandly, "you're afraid to have a wife at the wheel?"

"I'll risk it," he said, grinning back. "After all, if you wreck it, you can always replace it with a few trips to Reno or Vegas."

"Such an understanding husband," she drawled lovingly.

He stretched out a hand and found hers, squeezing it tightly for an instant before returning his fingers to the wheel. "My wife. My very own wife." He sounded dazzled by the notion.

He parked the Porsche in the drive of the house, which was perched high on a coast cliff, and took Alyssa's hand as they started up the flagstone walk. Just before they stepped through the door into the cedar-walled, modern home with its huge stone fireplace and warm, glowing wood interior, Jordan abruptly swung her off her feet and into his arms.

"What in the world?" she exclaimed, laughing as he carried her over the threshold.

"Bad luck not to carry a wife over the threshold," he informed her, kicking the door shut behind him.

"I keep telling you that for a mathematician the principle of 'luck' doesn't exist."

"I'll always have a touch of the gambler in me." He grinned unrepentantly, carrying her on into the living room and up the curved wooden staircase that led to the bedrooms.

The laughter went out of Alyssa's eyes as she looked up at him, her arms around his neck. "You don't feel as though marrying me was a...a risk, do you? That you're taking a chance?"

He halted at the top of the stairs and stared hungrily down into her face. "Alyssa, marrying you was the smartest, surest thing I've ever done in my life. I love you."

She touched his shoulder with her lips. "And I love you."

The tremor that went through him flowed into her, and by the time he had carried her into the wide bedroom and set her down on the fluffy comforter that covered the bed, Alyssa knew both of them were trembling with the force of their stirring passion. It would always be like this between them, she knew with great certainty. Passion and love and trust. With all of that going for them, they could face anything together.

Jordan stood beside the bed, drinking in the sight of her lying there wearing his ring. "I don't know how I survived as long as I did in my world waiting for you," he murmured.

Then he lowered himself slowly beside her, undoing the buttons of the neat champagne-colored jacket she had worn with a matching skirt for her wedding. Alyssa fumbled with his clothing as he undressed her. Her fingers were shaking, she realized in amazement. And so were his. That knowledge made her smile.

"Such good hands," she whispered dreamily as he slipped off her suit and then reluctantly sat up to remove the rest of his own clothing.

"My hands?" he pushed off his shoes and them came back down beside her, magnificently naked and passionately aroused. "Do you like my hands?" He touched her throat with his fingertips.

"I love your hands." She caught the tormenting fingers and drew them to her lips to kiss them warmly. He groaned at the delicate caress, leaning over her to kiss the hardening peaks of her breasts. Languidly, she arched against his mouth, and his tongue came out to stab excitingly.

With wonder and longing and deep passion, they built the fires between them. Jordan's sensitive fingers moved over Alyssa, rediscovering the exquisitely vulnerable places he had learned before and which he delighted in arousing. She felt the taut, waiting hardness of his thighs pressing against her hip and marveled at the fierceness of his desire for her. It made her feel more wanted and needed than she had ever felt in her life. She could give this man as much as he gave her, and the shared knowledge was a fundamental part of their passion.

Lovingly, she drew her fingers down his chest, tangling them briefly in the crisp, curling hair before going on to seek the hard planes of his thigh. There she clenched her nails tantalizingly and was rewarded by Jordan's low, muttered groan of desire.

"You have a way of teasing and tormenting me that nearly drives me out of my head!"

"Only nearly?" she mocked, and was instantly

punished when his own prowling fingers trailed unerringly to the heated, damp place between her legs. "Oh, Jordan!" Under the magic of his touch, she went wild, twisting against him and arching upward with feminine invitation and pleading.

She was so perfect, Jordan thought, gazing down at his new wife in wonder. She was everything he needed in this world, and he would take care of her no matter what. She would never have cause to regret marrying him. So sweet, so perfect and so full of love. How had he existed so long without love?

"You're so beautiful in my arms," he said, dropping a moist kiss on her stomach. "So warm and welcoming. You make me feel so loved."

"Oh, Jordan, that's exactly how you make me feel. No wonder we couldn't resist each other!" She feathered her hands along his shoulders and then wound them deeply into his hair, tugging him up and along her writhing body. "Make love to me, darling. I need you so much."

"I will, sweetheart, I will," he vowed. Tantalizingly, he drew his hair-roughened leg along the inside of her smooth one, and Alyssa moaned in response. When he felt her coffee-and cream-colored nails sink into his shoulders, he closed the distance between them a little further.

"Yes, Jordan, yes!"

"In a moment. In a moment." He buried his lips at her throat, inhaling the scent of her. His senses demanded that he take her completely, but he wanted to savor to the ultimate the delightful struggle she waged when she was urging him to her. He loved having her go wild beneath his hands.

Alyssa knew what he was doing, but she was helpless to react other than exactly as he wished. She arched her hips upward, straining to link her body to his. There! She could feel the heaviness of his manhood just there, only a small distance from her feminine core.

"Come to me, darling," she whispered in passionate enticement. "Come and make me yours."

As always, she won the delicious battle. Jordan gathered her to him, moving against her with power and need, taking her fully. And as always, in the process of taking, he was lost. The barriers between them fell completely, trapping them together in a swelling tide of love and desire.

Alyssa reveled in the glory of the claiming, knowing that the feeling was a shared one. She wrapped her smooth legs around the hard, muscled length of him, and her arms were laced tightly around his neck. Over and over again, she whispered his name. The shimmering spiral twisted higher, and they climbed it together, every movement of Jordan's body sending them to another level.

"Jordan!"

He heard the little crack in her voice, the one he was coming to know and love so well, the one that told him she was nearing her ultimate plateau. "Yes," he growled against her mouth. "Let it happen. Give yourself to me completely!"

The command seemed to send her over the edge. With a small cry, which Jordan drank from her mouth, Alyssa felt the indescribable release of the coiling tension in the depths of her loins. The primitive pleasure that was unlike anything else in the universe took her, sending rippling shivers through her body. Her nails left small half circles against the bronzed skin of Jordan's back, and when he felt the delicious sensation, he could no longer hold back his own surging satisfaction.

"Alyssa! My God, Alyssa!"

She clung to him as he crushed her deeply into the quilt, loving the heavy warmth of him as he gave himself up totally to the moment. When it was over, she stroked his back in long, lingering caresses, their legs entwined, his head beside hers on the pillow.

When she opened her eyes, he was watching her through lazily narrowed lids. "Hello, Mrs. Kyle."

"Hello," she whispered back, her mouth soft.

"I love you. I love having a wife. Do we get to call ourselves a family when there's only two of us?"

"I think so," Alyssa murmured gently. "Do you like the idea of being a family?"

"I love the idea. I love everything that includes you." He traced the outline of her lips with his forefinger.

"And besides, it sounds so respectable, doesn't it?" she mocked tenderly.

"Being able to say I have a wife gives me a curiously stable feeling. Like betting when you know exactly who's holding what at the table. Also," he went on with a teasing light in his eyes, "it solves the problem of who gets to toss the coin."

"What coin?"

"The one we were going to toss to see whether Chandler or Kyle came first in the name of our new consulting firm, remember?"

"Oh, that coin?" She frowned at him with mock ferocity. "Is that why you married me? So that there couldn't be any argument over my last name?"

"Well, if you want a double name now we'll have to call it Kyle-Kyle, won't we?" he returned ingenuously.

"I don't think that has quite the ring to it that Chandler-Kyle had," she observed dubiously.

"Well, we'll just settle on Kyle Consulting then, how's that?"

"Do I detect a note of masculine possessiveness in

all this? You have something against me using my own name?"

"How did you guess?" He picked up her hand, the one on which she wore his ring, and kissed the band of gold. "Now that I have you, I intend to spend the rest of my life making sure you never escape."

"Jordan," she murmured, spreading her fingers along his jaw. "I have no desire to escape."

"Oh, my sweet Alyssa," he murmured, shaking his head once in a gesture of wonder. "Do you realize how lucky we are to have found each other? Do you have any idea of the incredible good fortune it was for me that you wandered into that casino that night in Vegas?"

"I keep telling you that we probability experts don't believe in luck!" she drawled.

"And how many times do I have to tell you that we professional gamblers have a very healthy respect for it?"

She sighed laughingly. "I can see you're going to bring a unique perspective to the business world."

He propped himself up on one elbow and smiled down at her. "We still have that bottle of champagne and the paté to open, remember? We were supposed to come straight home from the minister's office and celebrate our wedding with a gourmet luncheon, as I recall."

"How could I forget! It's not my fault we wound up in bed instead of opening the paté and the champagne," she reminded him indignantly. "Now that you've exercised your privileges as a new husband, are you ready to go eat?"

He considered that for a long moment. "Actually, even though I'm getting hungry for food, I seem to be even hungrier for you."

She sat up beside him, eyes laughing. "Enough is enough, master! Let's go eat!" She tried to slide lithely off the side of the bed, but he snagged her wrist in an unshakable grip.

"Wait a second. We'll toss a coin and see which course of action we ought to follow," he suggested smoothly, hanging onto her while he leaned over the edge of the bed to rummage in the pocket of his slacks.

"Jordan, you're impossible," she informed him, amused.

"Call it," he ordered, flipping the coin into the air with an expert twist.

"Heads we go eat paté and drink champagne," she said quickly.

An instant later, the coin landed. Unable to resist, she leaned forward to see which way it had fallen.

"Tails," he announced grandly, showing her the evidence. "That means we stay here and satisfy this hunger first." He reached to pull her close, satisfaction and anticipation radiating from him.

"Do you always win?" Alyssa demanded just before his mouth closed over hers.

"Always."

* * * * *

REQUEST YOUR FREE BOOKS!

2 FREE NOVELS
FROM THE ROMANCE/SUSPENSE
COLLECTION PLUS 2 FREE GIFTS!

YES! Please send me 2 FREE novels from the Romance/Suspense Collection and my 2 FREE gifts. After receiving them, if I don't wish to receive any more books, I can return the shipping statement marked "cancel." If I don't cancel, I will receive 4 brand-new novels every month and be billed just $5.24 per book in the U.S., or $5.74 per book in Canada, plus 25¢ shipping and handling per book plus applicable taxes, if any*. That's a savings of at least 10% off the cover price! I understand that accepting the 2 free books and gifts places me under no obligation to buy anything. I can always return a shipment and cancel at any time. Even if I never buy another book from the Reader Service, the two free books and gifts are mine to keep forever.

185 MDN EF3H   385 MDN EF3J

Name	(PLEASE PRINT)
Address	Apt. #
City	State/Prov.	Zip/Postal Code

Signature (if under 18, a parent or guardian must sign)

Mail to The Reader Service:

IN U.S.A.	IN CANADA
P.O. Box 1867	P.O. Box 609
Buffalo, NY	Fort Erie, Ontario
14240-1867	L2A 5X3

Not valid to current subscribers to the Romance Collection,
the Suspense Collection or the Romance/Suspense Collection.

Want to try two free books from another line?
Call 1-800-873-8635 or visit www.morefreebooks.com.

* Terms and prices subject to change without notice. NY residents add applicable sales tax. Canadian residents will be charged applicable provincial taxes and GST. This offer is limited to one order per household. All orders subject to approval. Credit or debit balances in a customer's account(s) may be offset by any other outstanding balance owed by or to the customer. Please allow 4 to 6 weeks for delivery.

BOB206

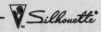
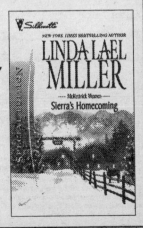